Lapland

Sweden

Jämtland

Norrbotten

Finland

Ångermanland   Västerbotten

Medelpad

Nils' journey through Sweden

Abridged version by Tage and Katyherine Aurell, 1962.
Edited and adapted by Rebecca Alsberg, 1989.
Translated by Joan Tate.

First published in Swedish under the title
Nils Holgerssons underbara resa genom Sverige
by Bonniers Junior Förlag AB, 1989
First published in English in 1992 by Floris Books
Fifth printing 2005

British Library CIP Data available

ISBN 0-86315-139-6

Printed in Denmark

The Wonderful Adventures of Nils

Selma Lagerlöf

Illustrated by Lars Klinting

Floris Books

Chapter 1

Once upon a time there was a boy. He was not up to much and mostly liked sleeping and eating and getting into mischief.

It was Sunday morning and the boy's parents were just off to church. Good, thought the boy, then I can go shooting with Father's gun without anyone interfering.

But his father probably guessed what he was thinking.

"If you don't want to come with us, then you must read the sermon at home," he said. Mother brought the book of sermons and opened it.

"Fourteen and a half pages," she said. And Father will question you on every single one. So start reading now if you're going to get through it all."

At last they set off. It was lovely and fresh outside and the trees were in bud, the water murmuring along all the ditches and the coltsfoot in full flower. Father and Mother would have enjoyed their walk to church if they hadn't had to think about their son. He was sluggish and lazy and didn't want to learn anything at school. He was also unkind to animals and people.

Back at home in the cottage, the boy started to read half aloud, but the mumbling made him sleepy and all of a sudden he nodded off.

But then a slight noise woke him up. Right in front of him in the window was a little mirror, and in it he saw the lid of Mother's best chest had been raised. A gnome was sitting on the edge of the chest looking delightedly down at all the fine things inside.

The boy was very surprised, but he was not afraid of anyone so small. It might be fun to play a trick on the little fellow, so he grabbed the fly-net and in a flash had caught the gnome in it. The gnome lay at the bottom pleading to be let out.

"I have been good to you for many years," he said.

"If you let me go, I'll give you a silver spoon and a gold coin."

The boy agreed to that, but just as the gnome was about to climb out, it occurred to him that he could have asked for greater wealth, so he started shaking the net to make the gnome fall back into it. At the same moment, the boy received such a terrible clip over the ear, he thought his head would split open, and he fell senseless to the floor.

When he woke, he was alone again. The lid of the chest was down and the fly-net back in its place. But his cheek was burning hot, so it had been no dream.

But what was this? The cottage seemed to have grown. He had to climb up on to the chair, and in order to see over the edge of the table, he had to get up on to the arm. And to read, he had to get right into the middle of the book itself.

He read a few lines, then happened to look at himself in the mirror.

"Look!" he cried.

"There's another gnome!" Because he could see quite clearly a little fellow in trousers and a pixie cap.

"He's dressed just like me," said the boy, clapping his hands. But then he saw that the boy in the mirror was imitating him. He pinched his arm and scratched his head and at once the boy in the mirror did the same. The boy ran round to the back of the mirror to see if anyone was hiding there, but he found no one, and then he really was frightened. He realized now that the gnome had put a spell on him and the little fellow in the mirror was himself.

If I wait a while, I'll probably soon be a human again, he thought, closing his eyes. But no! He stayed just as small.

"I must make it up with the gnome again," he exclaimed and started searching for him behind the cupboard and under the sofa, but he found no gnome. The boy started crying and pleading, and he promised never to play tricks again, never to be unkind and never to fall asleep over the sermon. As long as he became human again, he would be good and hardworking and obedient.

But that didn't help in the slightest.

Perhaps he could catch the gnome out in the cowshed? The door of the cottage was open a crack, so he slipped out through it, and on the steps outside he found a tiny little pair of clogs. The gnome must have thought this wretched business was going to last a long time.

When the boy came out on to the farmyard, a flock of sparrows caught sight of him and started cheeping.

"Look, look, look at Nils Gooseboy! Look at Tom Thumb! Nils Holgersson Thumb!" Then there was a terrible cackling.

"Cockadoodledoo," crowed the cock. "Serve him right, he who pulls my coxcomb."

"Cluck-cluck-cluck," shrieked the hens. "Serve him right. Serve him right!"
The boy listened with astonishment.

"I suppose I understand what they're saying because I've been turned into a gnome," he mumbled thoughtfully.

He threw a stone at the hens and shouted: "Shut up, you rabble!" But the hens weren't afraid of him any longer and they didn't quieten down until the cat came creeping along.

"Puss," said the boy. "Please, tell me where the gnome is."

The cat seemed to be in a good mood and said in a soft voice: "Oh, yes, I know where the gnome lives." But then a glint came into his eye and he added: "Am I perhaps supposed to help you because you've pulled my tail so often?"

That made the boy angry and he quite forgot he was so small.

"I'll pull your tail again!" he shouted and ran straight at the cat. The cat leapt at once, knocking him over and putting his claws on his chest, his mouth open and hissing, his eyes as red as fire. The boy thought his last moment had come and cried out for help. But no one came. In the end the cat let him go.

"There you are," he said. "Now you can see which of us is stronger." And he padded away looking as pious as when he had come.

From inside the cowshed came the bellowing and stamping of thirty cows.

"Moo! It's good there's still some justice in the world," lowed Mayrose as the boy stepped inside. Again he tried asking after the gnome.

"Just you come over here," said Star. "Then you can dance on my horns."

"Come over here and I'll pay you back for that wasp you put into my ear!" snapped Lily.

"Come over here and I'll pay you back for all the times you've pulled away the milking stool from under your mother, and all the times you've tripped her up when she was carrying the milk pail, and all the tears she has shed for you," bellowed Mayrose, the eldest and the most angry with him.

The boy wanted to say he was sorry and he would never be anything else but good if they told him where the gnome was. But they just shook their heads and tossed their horns. Just as well if he slipped away from there.

When he got outside he felt really rather downhearted, for he realized no one on the farm was going to help him find the gnome, nor would it be much use if he did manage to find him.

He clambered up on to the wide stone wall that ran round the farm and sat down to think. What would happen if he didn't go back to being human again? What would Mother and Father think when they came back from church? Well, the whole village would wonder.

He was terribly unhappy. Just imagine, he was no longer a human being, but an odd little creature who couldn't play with other boys, who wouldn't inherit the farm from his parents and certainly would never find a girl to marry him.

He looked at his home, small and poor in other people's eyes perhaps, but to him it was all too good. He would have to live in a little hole somewhere under the cowshed floor. And he would never again be happy about anything.

Chapter 2

It was a wonderfully beautiful day and Nils had never seen the sky so blue as the migratory birds came racing by. They had flown over the Baltic Sea and were heading north. They must have been all kinds of birds, but the only ones he recognized were the wild geese flying in two long lines in the shape of a plough. He could hear them calling up there: "On to the mountains! On to the mountains!"

The wild geese suddenly caught sight of the tame geese down on the farm and they flew closer to the ground and cried: "Come with us! Come with us! To the mountains, to the mountains!"

But the tame geese sensibly replied: "Things are quite fine for us here."

Yes, it was an unusually lovely day and it must have been a great joy to fly through the air. So for every new skein of wild geese flying by, the tame geese grew more and more uneasy and flapped and flapped their wings as if they wished to leave too.

"What madness!" said the old mother goose. "That lot will soon be both hungry and cold."

However, in one of the young ganders the cries from the wild geese had aroused an uncontrollable desire to travel. When another skein flew by and called "Come with us, come with us!" he replied: "Wait, wait! I'm coming."

He spread out his wings and tried to rise, but he was so unused to flying, he fell to the ground again.

The wild geese turned and flew more slowly to see if he would have another try.

Nils Gooseboy saw and heard all this as he lay there on the stone wall.

"It would be terrible if the gander flew away," he said to himself. "It would upset Mother and Father greatly if he'd gone when they came back from church."

Again he quite forgot he was small and helpless. He jumped down right into the middle of the flock of geese and flung his arms round the gander's neck.

"Don't you go flying away," he cried.

But at that very moment the gander had found out how to take off from the ground, and now he couldn't stop and shake off the boy, so Nils had to go with him up into the air.

Everything happened so quickly, it took his breath away. Before he had even thought of letting go the gander's neck, they were so high up he would have been killed if he had fallen to the ground. All he could do was to wriggle his way up on to the gander's back. Even then it was no easy task hanging on to that slippery back between those sweeping wings. He had to thrust both hands deep down into feathers so as not to fall off.

Nils grew so dizzy that for a long while he didn't know where he was, the air whistling and hissing round him and roaring in the feathers like a proper storm, thirteen geese flapping and cackling all round him. In the end he came to his senses enough to realize he ought to find out where the geese were taking him. But he didn't dare look down, for he would surely turn giddy if he tried.

Yet the wild geese were flying fairly low because their new travelling companion couldn't breathe in the thin air higher up, so for his sake they flew a little more slowly than usual.

Gradually the boy made himself glance down in the direction of the earth. To him it seemed as if a large cloth had been laid out beneath him and divided up into an incredible number of large and small squares, corners and straight edges everywhere, nothing round or crooked.

"What kind of chequered cloth is that?" he said to himself, not expecting anyone to reply. But the wild geese at once cried: "Fields and meadows! Fields and meadows!"

He was racing across the flat plain of Skåne. The bright green squares were fields of rye that had been sown the autumn before and had stayed green beneath the snow. The yellowish grey ones were stubble fields, the brown ones clover and the dark squares pastures or ploughed fields. Some dark squares with grey in the middle were farms, the green squares their gardens.

The boy couldn't help laughing. He had always liked riding fast and wildly, but he had never before known such a speed as this. And he had never thought it could be so fresh and free as it was up here in the air, and what a good smell of soil and resin could rise from the earth. Being carried along as high as this was like flying away from all his troubles and annoyances.

The great tame gander was very proud and happy as he flew over the plain of Skåne in the company of the wild geese. But as the day wore on, he began to tire and fell several goose-lengths behind the others.

Then the goose flying last called to the leader goose at the front: "Akka, Akka from Kebnekajse! The white one is falling behind."

"Tell him it's much easier to fly more quickly than slowly," replied the leader goose, and went on as before.

The gander did try, but he grew more and more exhausted and started sinking.

"Akka, Akkka from Kebnekajse, the white one is falling!"

"Anyone who can't keep up should turn round and go home!" cried Akka, not slowing down in the slightest.

Oh, so that's how it is, thought the gander. They had tempted him to go with them just for fun and they had no intention of taking him to Lapland. Then he wouldn't be able to show these tramps that a tame goose could also do a thing or two. That annoyed him in particular, because he had known about Akka from Kebnekajse before. Although he was a domestic goose, he had nevertheless heard about this leader goose who was over a hundred years old. She was very much respected, but more than anything else, she and her flock despised the tame geese. He would have liked to show them that he was their equal. Then suddenly the little fellow on his back said: "Please, Martin, you must see that you, who've never flown before, can't possibly go with them all the way up to Lapland. Turn back before you wear yourself out!"

Did the wretch think he couldn't manage? The gander could think of nothing worse than this stripling, and he was so annoyed now, he decided he would stick it out.

"If you say another word, I'll throw you off!" he hissed and flew on almost as fast as the others.

But now the sun was sinking fast and the geese set off downwards. Before the boy and the gander knew where they were, they were standing on the shores of Lake Vomb. The great lake was almost covered with a thin layer of ice full of holes and cracks, and round the ice ran a belt of gleaming black water. Where the geese had landed was a pine forest with frozen snow beneath the bushy prickly branches.

The boy was so agitated, he wanted to cry out aloud. He was hungry. He hadn't eaten anything all day. And where would he get food from? Who would find him somewhere to sleep, warm him and protect him from wild animals?

The forest started rustling and creaking, fear creeping up in the wake of the dusk, the happy mood he had been in up there in the air now gone.

In his anxiety, he looked around for his travelling companion, for he had no one else to be with.

But the gander was lying quite still as if dying, his neck drooping and his eyes closed, and the boy who had previously been so unkind to animals now grew terribly afraid of losing the gander. He started pushing him to get him down to the water, though the gander was large and heavy, so the boy had to use all his strength, but at last the gander slid into the water head first. His beak soon appeared out of the water and he snorted, then swam away out towards the reeds. When he turned back again he had a little perch in his beak.

"Here you are, in thanks for helping me," he said.

It was the first time for a long time the boy had heard a friendly word and he was just as pleased about that as he was about the raw fish. At first he thought it was probably impossible to eat, but then he felt like trying all the same. His sheath knife was no bigger than a matchstick, but it was good enough for scaling the fish, and it wasn't long before the perch had all gone.

"It would have been to my credit if I could have gone with them to Lapland and shown them that even a tame goose can manage," the gander said when the boy had swallowed the very last bit. "But I can't manage on my own on such a long journey. Would you come with me and help? I will take you back home again in the autumn."

The boy thought they ought to turn back as soon as possible, though of course it would be good to escape having to face Mother and Father for a little while longer. He was about to answer yes when all the wild geese came soaring up from the lake in one long line, the leader goose at the head. They were much smaller than the tame goose and their feathers were grey with a touch of brown. Their yellow eyes shone as if a fire were burning inside them, and it was clear from their big feet that they never asked what they were trampling on.

They dipped their necks and the gander did the same, then they stood for a long time greeting each other. Finally, the leader goose said: "May we hear what kind of creature you are who wants to be with the wild geese? You're not much good at flying. But perhaps you can swim and run?"

"My name's Martin and I come from West Vemmenhög. I can't run and I have never swum further than across a ditch. But I want to show you that we tame geese are also quite capable," replied the gander, although he was now sure the leader goose would take him with them.

"You answer bravely, so perhaps you can become a good travelling companion. Stay with us for a few days and then we can see what you can do. But who is it you have with you? Is he from the gnome family?"

Martin did not want to reveal that the boy was human.

"His name's Tom Thumb and he's a gooseherd. He'd probably be useful to have on the journey."

Great age had made the leader goose grey and worn, but her eyes shone more clearly and somehow more youthfully than the eyes of the others. She said grandly: "I am Akka from Kebnekajse. Over there are Yksi from Vassijaure and Kaksi from Nuolja. And these are Kolme, Neljä, Viisi and Kuusi. The other six goslings are also mountain geese from the very best families. We don't share our sleeping places with anyone who doesn't say what family he comes from."

The boy quickly stepped forward and bowed.

"I am Nils Holgersson and until today I was a human being. But this morning ..."

The wild geese immediately started back three steps, hissing angrily: "Get away from here! We can't stand human beings!"

"Surely you aren't afraid of a little creature like that?" said the gander to keep the peace.

The leader goose was obviously finding it difficult to hide her terror.

"I have learnt to fear all human beings," she said. "But if you stand guarantor for this one, then he can stay the night with us. We're going to sleep on that ice out there."

"You're wise to choose such a safe place to sleep in," said Martin, refusing to be scared away. "But tomorrow I'll be leaving you, for I've promised not to abandon him."

"Do as you like," said Akka, and she flew out on to the ice, all the wild geese following her and settling down with their beaks under their wings.

The boy was both appalled and afraid, but all Martin said was: "Gather up some brushwood and dry grass, as much as you can carry."

When the boy had his arms full, the gander took him in his beak and flew out on to the ice. He then settled on to the dry grass so as not to freeze to the ice, and pushed the boy under his wing.

"You'll be comfortable there," he said. The next moment, the boy was fast asleep, he was so tired — but he was warm and cosy.

Chapter 3

Nils was woken suddenly by Martin striking out with a wing. The boy fell down on the ice and sat there, drowsy as he was, the geese all flapping and shrieking round him. He couldn't make out what was happening until he saw a small long-legged dog sneaking away with a goose in its mouth. The boy at once rushed over the ice after it, and although it was quite dark, he could easily see all the cracks and holes, because now he had the good night vision of a gnome.

The ice floe had floated back towards the shore again and that was the way the dog had come. Nils ran the same way and came to a large beech wood. He shouted at the dog to drop its prey, but it was no dog. It was Smirre the fox, a truly great robber feared all over the area.

In the end, the boy managed to catch hold of the fox's tail, but for a long way Smirre pulled him along with him. When the fox saw that his pursuer was harmless, he stopped to tease him a little. But the boy pulled as hard as he could, so Smirre had to let go and the goose was suddenly able to flap off and disappear.

The fox was terribly angry and swung round, making the leaves swirl, but the boy had kept his hold on the tail and hung on laughing, though he was afraid the fox might grab him, so he quickly let go his tail and clambered up a tree. Smirre went on scampering round until he discovered the boy up in the tree, and he sat down to wait below.

It was a terribly cold night and Nils didn't dare sleep in case he fell down. At last the sun rose and the cries of the wild geese came from over by the lake. I suppose they think the fox has eaten me up now, he thought, and they won't even bother to look for me. He was close to tears.

After a while, a lone wild goose came flying under the thick ceiling of branches. Smirre crept up to her and took a great leap. Again and again he leapt, but each

time the goose flew away, just like a lively dance moving further and further away, then suddenly the goose had gone. When the fox came panting back to the tree, the little fellow had also flown away.

The wild geese continued their journey over the mansions and manor farms of Skåne, over parks and wide fields where they could graze. One day they stopped for a while by Lake Vomb and the wild geese challenged Martin at all kinds of sporting competitions. They all laughed and enjoyed themselves, Nils most of all.

"But you run around far too recklessly," Akka said to him. "Remember you have a great many enemies. The fox and the pine marten in the forest, the otter on the lake shore, the weasel along the fencing and the adder in the forest meadows." And out on the fields he had to think about hawks and falcons, eagles and buzzards not to mention magpies and crows and owls.

The boy was not all that frightened of dying, but he had no wish whatsoever to be eaten up.

"What can I do to protect myself?" he asked. With so many enemies after his life, it seemed quite impossible.

"Keep in with the little animals of the forest," Akka advised him. "They can warn you of the dangers and find hiding places for you."

But when the boy asked Sirle the squirrel for help, he abruptly said no.

"Ho, ho," he said. "You're Nils Gooseboy, who pulled down the swallow's nest, smashed the starling's eggs and put squirrels in a cage. You can help yourself now, and be glad we don't chase you off home again."

Oh, supposing the wild geese found out how unkind he had been before! Just when he was trying to be so good in every way so that Akka wouldn't desert him. But in the evening he was told that Sirle's wife had been kidnapped and that her four newborn babies were starving to death. He must help them and show what he was worth!

The children on a nearby farm had captured Mrs Sirle and put her in a cage. They thought she would be fun to look at, but the squirrel sat miserably in a corner, refusing to eat anything. That night, a little fellow crept into the farm with a tiny bundle in his arms and pushed it in to the mother squirrel. Four times he ran back and forth, and when morning came, the people on the farm found to their amazement the squirrel had all her babies with her in the cage.

"We should be ashamed of ourselves," said the father on the farm. He took the squirrels out of the cage and put them into his eldest daughter's apron.

"Take them out to the hazel grove now and give them back their freedom."

That day, the chaffinches in all the thickets sang about Nils Gooseboy's heroic deed. There was such a chatter, Akka was bound to hear them.

A whole week had gone by since the boy had been bewitched and he was still just as small. He wondered what he would do when the wild geese continued on north. Just as he was sitting there pondering, Akka and the others came over to him, and they were walking in such a dignified way, he immediately realized he was now going to be told what they had decided.

"You must be wondering," said Akka, "why I haven't thanked you for saving one of us from Smirre the fox. But deeds are better than words. I have sent a message to the gnome who put a spell on you and told him how well you are behaving here with us, and how resourceful you were when helping Sirle's wife. He says that you can go home straightaway and become human again."

At first the boy was pleased. But then his mood changed.

He was thinking about adventures and freedom and fun and journeys under the sky, and he wailed with misery.

"I don't care about being human!" he said. "I want to go with you to Lapland."

"But that gnome is so easily annoyed," said Akka. "If you say no now, I may find it difficult to persuade him later."

The strange thing about Nils Holgersson was that he had never really liked anyone, not his father and mother, nor his teacher at school, nor his schoolfriends. So there was no one he missed or longed for.

"I want to go with you to Lapland. That's why I've been so good for a whole week," he sobbed.

"I won't say no," said Akka. "But there may come a day when you bitterly regret it."

"No," said the boy. "I've never had such a good time as I have with you. There's nothing to regret."

"Then it shall be as you wish," said Akka.

Nils was so happy, he had to weep with joy just as he had previously been weeping with sorrow.

Chapter 4

Early one morning, the geese sleeping out on the ice on Lake Vomb were woken by loud cries from the air.

"Triroop, triroop! Trianut the crane greets Akka to say that tomorrow the great crane dance is to be held on Kullaberg. Welcome!"

The wild geese were very pleased. "You're lucky to be able to see the crane dance," they told the gander.

"Is it so remarkable?" said Martin.

"It's what you've never even dreamt of!" the wild geese replied.

"But first we must go and get some food," said Akka. They flew to the marshlands south of Glimmingehus. The old stone fortress was so high and vast that it could be seen for miles around on the plain, and a stork had built its nest on the very top of its ridged roof.

When the wild geese had had their fill of meadow grass, they flew straight to the assembly of animals and the crane dance.

Kullaberg was a long low mountain that had rushed out into the sea as far as it could get, its steep cliffs richly sculpted by water and wind, and on the flat mountain top were forests and fields, heather-covered heathlands and bare stone.

Since time immemorial, the creatures had gathered there every year on a playground well hidden behind hills and hillocks. Each species of animal kept to its own hill, although, of course, peace reigned among them all during the assembly. On that day a little hare could walk over the foxes' hill without losing as much as one of its long ears.

The boy let his gaze roam from hill to hill. On one he could see the many-spiked antlers of the deer, on another the crests on the heads of the grey herons. One hill was red with foxes, another black and white with sea birds and another brown with hares.

The sun rose, a cloud appearing in the sky above the playground, and suddenly the whole sky began twittering and singing as if consisting of nothing but notes. In the end, the whole singing cloud came down on to a hill that became completely covered with grey larks, colourful red, grey and white chaffinches, speckled starlings and green and yellow titmice. After them came a great heavy bluish grey cloud no ray of the sun could penetrate, gloomy and frightening it was, and full of cries and noises, mocking laughter and the most ominous cawing. Everyone was glad when the cloud at last dissolved into a shower of crows and jackdaws, ravens and rooks.

The games soon began. A hundred capercaillies in brilliant black and brown attire and bright red eyes hurtled up into a large oak tree. They raised their tails to show their white protective feathers, and deep down in their throats began the gurgling.

"Tik-up, tik-up," they went, then "Siss, siss, siss, listen so lovely it is, siss, siss." They all went into raptures, beside themselves, and their ecstasy also seemed to infect all the other animals.

Just as the black cocks with their beautifully curved tail feathers rushed out on to the playground to compete with the capercaillies, something terrible happened. A fox came creeping quite slowly up on to the wild geese's hill. He was walking very carefully and was quite far up the slope before anyone noticed.

But then a goose spotted him and as she couldn't believe a fox had crept in among the geese with any good intentions, she started calling: "Watch out, wild geese, watch out!" The fox grabbed her by the neck, perhaps largely to quieten her, but the wild geese had already heard her and flew high up into the air. From up there they saw Smirre the fox on their hill with a dead goose in his mouth.

But Smirre had shattered the peace of the day and for that he was duly punished. He was at once surrounded by a crowd of foxes and sentenced according to ancient custom. Whoever disturbs the peace on the great day of games must go into exile. For the rest of his life he would regret he had been unable to leave Akka and her flock alone.

So Smirre was forbidden to stay in Skåne and was banished from his wife and family, from his hunting grounds, his resting places and hiding places, and had to try his luck in foreign parts. And so that all foxes in Skåne should know that Smirre was outlawed from the countryside, the eldest of the foxes bit off the tip of his right ear. As soon as this was done, the young foxes threw themselves at Smirre and all he could do was to flee, so with all the young foxes at his heels, he fled away from Kullaberg.

At that moment a whisper ran from hill to hill: "Look, the cranes are coming ..."

Then came the grey twilight-clad birds with their plumed wings and red feather jewels on their heads. Long-legged, with slender necks and small heads, they glided down the slope, half flying, half dancing, moving with unimaginable speed and delight, as if grey shadows were playing a game the eye was scarcely able to follow, as if they had learnt from the mists that hover over solitary mosses. There was magic in it, and all those who had not been to Kullaberg before realized just why the whole assembly bore the name of the dance of the cranes. There was wildness in it, but the feeling it gave rise to was still a wonderful yearning. No one gave a thought to fighting any more. Instead they all wanted to rise up above the clouds and float towards the supernatural, leaving their burdensome bodies that dragged them down to earth.

The animals felt this yearning for the unattainable only once a year and that was the day when they saw the great dance of the cranes.

Chapter 5

The same day as the wild geese left Lake Vomb, the rain came, and when the first showers spattered against the ground, the little birds let out such squeals of joy, the boy jumped as he sat there on the gander's back.

"Now we'll have some rain! Rain brings flowers and leaves, then there'll be insects and larvae and lots of food for us!" the birds sang. The wild geese were also pleased, because the rain made holes in the ice on the lakes, so they too responded with cheerful calls. But then the sky turned evenly grey, the rain hammering heavily on their wings and making its way between their oiled outer feathers right through to their bodies. The ground was hidden by the wet mist and everything merged in dark confusion. The geese were silent and the boy was shivering with cold.

But he kept his spirits up, and when the wild geese landed on a moss, he ran off in a cheerful mood to look for cranberries and frozen whortleberries. But in the evening, the wilderness turned horrible, rustling and swishing, and he was very cold and wet. He couldn't sleep under the gander's wing and felt he must have a fire and warmth if he were not to die of shivering.

He had caught a glimpse of a village as the geese had landed, so he slipped away in that direction. The village street was neatly planted with trees and the houses were painted in bright colours. He could hear people talking and laughing inside the warm cottages. But he didn't dare knock on any doors, for what would they say when they saw him?

Tears were not far away, and for the first time he was worried about shutting himself off from people.

He walked past the village store. Outside it was a plough and for a moment he sat down on it, dreaming he was at home with his mother and father. Then he roamed past the apothecary and the doctor's house, past the church and the post office, the school and all the shops. The further he went, the more he liked human beings and everything they were able to do. He was suddenly very frightened of never again being human.

What should he do? He sat down on some steps in the pouring rain and thought.

"It's too difficult for someone who has learnt as little as I have," he sighed. "Perhaps the pastor and the doctor and the teacher have a remedy for me. I shall go and ask them at once."

Then an owl appeared and perched in a nearby tree. A tawny owl under the eaves called out: "Twooit, Marsh Owl. How were things for you in foreign parts?"

"Fine, thanks. And what's been happening here at home?"

"Well, just imagine, a boy in Skåne has been turned into a gnome, and now he's travelling on a tame gander up to Lapland."

"Amazing, Tawny Owl! Won't he ever be a human again?"

"It's a secret, but the gnome has said that if the boy looks after the gander so that he comes back unharmed ... ssh, let's fly up into the church tower. Maybe someone's listening here on the village street."

The owls flew away and the boy threw his cap high up into the air.

"Hurrah! I'll be a human again. And of course I'll look after the gander. Hurrah! Hurrah!" In a happy mood, he hurried off back to the moss and his travelling companions.

Akka had sent Yksi and Kaksi north first to find out about the ice on all the waters and the snow on the land. On their return, Akka decided they were to fly towards the coast where spring comes early.

Neither the wild geese nor Smirre the fox thought they would ever meet again after they had left Skåne. But it so happened that the wild geese now took the route over Blekinge and that was where Smirre had also gone.

So one day when Smirre was hunting in a desolate stretch of forest, he caught sight of a flock of geese in flight. One goose was white, so he knew which they were. He at once set off after them, for not only did he want a good meal, but he also wanted revenge on them for all his vexations. But Akka had found a well-protected place to sleep on a narrow strip of shore, where no fox could get at them. In front of them rushed the River Ronneby and behind them was a steep mountain wall, where there were hawthorns and elders, rowans and willows with overhanging branches to hide the whole flock.

But Nils didn't dare sleep, all the same, the fear of the wilderness coming over him in the darkness. As he lay there under the gander's wing, he was unable to hear whether danger was approaching.

He thrust out his head and suddenly saw an eye glimmering among the bare branches. It was a pine marten creeping up on the geese. The boy seized a stone and flung it at the pine marten, which was so surprised it fell plop into the water, making such a splash, all the geese flew up with a crashing of wingbeats.

Akka followed the river down to Djupafors, where she found another place to sleep. In the whirlpools below the waterfall was a large flat rocky stone, and no fox or pine marten would ever dare to go there. The geese soon fell asleep, but the boy sat up to keep watch over the gander.

Through the roar of the water, he suddenly thought he heard a strange noise. When he turned round, he saw the head and paw of an otter just about to climb up on to the stone slab. He quickly drew out his sheath-knife and struck at the paw. The otter lost its foothold and vanished with a splash into the rapids. Once again they had to leave and find another place to sleep.

They flew south, and in the moonlight, Akka spotted a deserted spa hotel. They landed there on a balcony where it was probably safe, but all the same, the boy stayed awake and sat looking out over the sea, at islands and skerries, bays and straits.

Then he heard a horrible howl from the bath-house grounds and down there in the white moonlight he saw a fox! Smirre had followed the geese all night, but here it was impossible to reach them, so he couldn't help howling with rage.

"Is that you, Smirre?" called Nils.

"Yes, what do you think of the night I've arranged for you?"

"Oh, so it was you who set the pine marten and the otter on to us?" said Akka.

"Yes, it was. And now I'm going to play the fox-and-geese game with you wild geese. As long as one of you is alive, I'll follow you all over the country unless you throw that Tom Thumb down to me."

"I'll never give you Tom Thumb," said Akka.

"If you're that fond of him" said Smirre furiously, "then he'll be the first I'll take revenge on." Then he disappeared with an angry screech.

The boy was still awake, but this time it was Akka's words to the fox that were preventing him from sleeping. Never would he have believed he would hear anything so marvellous as someone wanting to risk her life for his sake.

And from that moment on, it could no longer be said of Nils Holgersson that he did not like anyone.

Karlskrona naval base lay deserted in the moonlight when the geese came flying over the archipelago, still searching for a safe sleeping place away from Smirre the fox. The boy thought what he could see was a giant stretching his arms up to the heights and whales and sharks and other great sea monsters were swimming on the milky white sea. But when they were nearer, he realized the giant was a church with two towers. The sea creatures were ships and the boy wanted to take a closer look at those when it grew light. The geese landed on one of the church towers and at last the boy dared to creep under the gander's wing. But he had slept for only five minutes when he slid out from under the wing and climbed down to the ground.

Fortunately there were no people in the market square, only a bronze statue of a man with a stern face, a broad nose and a large mouth, and a stick in his hand. The boy at once felt small and feeble, so tried to pluck up his courage by being witty.

"What's that funny fellow doing here?" he said loudly as he continued on across the square. Then he heard heavy footsteps tramping over the cobblestones, making the ground tremble and the houses shake. The boy was frightened. Is it really the bronze man walking? he thought, turning into a side street, but the bronze man came after him. Outside a little wooden church, a man was standing beckoning. The boy was pleased and rushed over to him, but then he saw that he was made of wood. Recently painted, he stood glistening in the moonlight, holding a board.

Oh, so it was only a poor-box ... and now the bronze man wasn't far away!

With your coin
help the poor

And of blessings
be sure

~ o ~

27

At that moment, the wooden man bent down towards the boy and held out his broad hand. As he could only think well of him, the boy leapt up into it and the wooden man tucked him under his hat. His arm was only just back in place when the bronze man stopped and said in a resounding voice: "And who are you?"

The wooden man raised his arm in a salute so that the old woodwork creaked. "Rosenbom, if I may say so, Your Majesty. First Boatswain on the ship of the line *Boldness*, then churchwarden and nowadays a poor-box, carved in wood."

The boy started when he heard the words "Your Majesty." So the statue was of no less than King Karl XI, the founder of the town.

"Have you seen a young scamp running around here tonight? If I catch the cheeky rascal, I'll teach him some manners!" said the King angrily, thumping his stick.

"Maybe so," replied the wooden man. "He probably ran down to the shipyard and hid."

"Then you come with me, Rosenbom. Four eyes see better than two," said the bronze man, and the wooden man realized the King would not take no for an

answer.

Huge and terrible, they strode through the streets of Karlskrona, the boy peeping out through a crack in the wooden man's hat. The King kicked open the gateway to the shipyard and the great wide harbour, where the big warships lay at anchor. So I wasn't all that silly to think they looked like sea monsters, thought the boy.

The bronze man and the wooden man walked round the shipyard quite forgetting to look for the boy, and like two old seadogs, enjoying what they saw. Finally they came to the yard where the figureheads from the old ships of the line were arrayed. The boy had never seen such an amazing sight before, those mighty terrifying faces, filled with proud daring. Then the bronze man said: "Take off your hat, Rosenbom! All these have been in battles for our fatherland!"

Without thinking, Rosenbom raised his wooden hat and cried: "I raise my hat to the King who chose this harbour and recreated the fleet!"

"Thank you, Rosenbom. You're a fine man! But what's this now?" For there was Nils Holgersson standing right in the middle of Rosenbom's bald head, raising his cap and in his turn crying: "Hurrah for you, funny fellow!"

The bronze man thumped the ground with his stick, but the boy never found out what he intended to do, because at that moment the sun rose and both the bronze man and the wooden man both vanished as if they had been mist. While the boy was still staring after them, the wild geese flew up from the church tower and hovered over the town, then suddenly the white gander spotted Nils Holgersson, swooped down out of the sky and picked him up.

Chapter 6

The wild geese flew out to a skerry to graze. Some grey geese they came across were very surprised to see their kinsfolk so far out on the outskirts of the archipelago, for wild geese usually fly inland.

Akka told them about Smirre the fox, and a wise old grey goose said: "It was a great misfortune for you that the fox was outlawed from his own country. Now he will persecute you all the way up to Lapland. Take the outer route to Öland and

stay there a few days so that Smirre loses track of you."

Akka considered that good advice. None of them had ever been to Öland before, but the grey geese said all they had to do was to fly south until they came to the great flight of birds. All birds heading for Finland and Russia rested on Öland, so there were plenty of signposts.

It was as calm and warm as a summer day, grand weather for a sea journey. Beyond the islands, the sea spread out so mirror-smooth, the boy thought the water had vanished. He had sky and clouds both above and below him when he first sat there — it felt as if he might fall in either direction, and it grew even worse when they reached the great flight of birds. Thousands of birds were flying as if along a staked-out route: ducks, velvet scoters, guillemots, long-tailed ducks, grebes, shrikes, oyster catchers and many many more. The boy could see the whole procession of birds reflected in the water, but he was so dizzy he thought the birds were all flying belly upwards. The birds were also so tired, they were quite silent, and that made everything unreal. Perhaps we're going all the way up to heaven, he thought, wondering what he would see there.

Then there was a crackle of shots, small white columns of smoke rising and the sound of agitated birds calling out: "Guns! Guns in the boats! Fly high!"

Oh no, they certainly weren't in heaven. A long line of boats full of marksmen lay down there, shot after shot echoing and dark little bodies sinking down towards the sea, cries of dismay rising from the others as they made their way up as fast as they could. The wild geese were safe, but the boy was dismayed. To think that anyone should want to shoot at Akka and Yksi and Kaksi. People didn't know what they were doing ...

A faint wind with great masses of white smoke in it soon came towards them, billowing more and more thickly. The birds grew agitated, but it was a great wet fog enveloping them, so thick they couldn't see a goose-length ahead of them. The other birds knew the way perfectly well, so started playing in the mist to lure each other astray. But they all knew where Öland was. It was much worse for the wild geese and they were tricked over and over again until even Akka's head was whirling.

"Where are you heading?" called a swan. "Come with me, I'll show you the right way." And after he had lured them far away from the others, he disappeared into the mist.

"Can't you see you're flying upside down?" cried a duck, and the boy flung his arms round the gander's neck in terror.

Then they heard a dull rumbling shot in the distance and Akka at once stretched out her neck, flapped her wings hard and set off at top speed. The old grey goose had told her that on the outermost point of the southern headland of Öland there was a cannon people fired off at the fog. Now that Akka knew the direction, no one in the world could tempt her astray.

On the southernmost tip of the island of Öland was a royal estate called Ottenby, a large estate that ran from shore to shore with a long wall separating the land from the rest of the island. The estate had always been a refuge for huge numbers of creatures, and in the spring and late summer, thousands of migrating birds came down to rest on the marshy shores below the great meadow.

When the wild geese had at last found their way to Öland, they also landed just there. The mist was still thick over the island, but the boy was astonished by all the birds he could distinguish on only one little stretch of the shore. Ducks and grey geese were grazing on the meadow and divers were fishing in the sea, the liveliest movement out on the long seaweed beds where the birds crowded together to feed on larvae. The boy walked around gazing at swans and sandpipers and shelducks. He had never been so close to them before.

The next morning was just as misty. The boy walked along the edge of the shore collecting mussels. Just as well to have some food with me, too, he thought. But he needed something to carry them in, so he found some old sedge grass tough and strong enough to weave it into a knapsack. That took him several hours, but then he was pleased with what he had done.

At midday, all the geese came running up crying: "The big white gander has vanished in the mist." The boy was terribly frightened.

"Have you seen a fox or a man or anything else dangerous?" he asked them. No, they had seen nothing. The gander had probably got lost in the mist.

The boy immediately set out to look for him.

"Martin! Martin! Where are you?" he called. He went on searching until darknes began to fall, but in vain. What would happen to him if he couldn't find Martin?

No one in the world could replace his friend the gander.

He walked miserably back across the meadow, but what was that white something appearing out of the mist but the gander!

"I've been wandering around lost all day," he said apologetically.

"Never leave me again, promise me," begged the boy, throwing his arms round Martin's neck.

"No, never, I promise you," said the gander.

But the next morning the geese came rushing over calling out that he had gone again! He must have got lost in the mist like the last time. And again Nils set off calling and searching, first along the shore and then inland right across to the windmills in the middle of the island, only to return in the evening, tired and worried, and this time he could only think that his travelling companion was lost for ever.

Then he heard the rattle of a stone falling and thought he could make out something moving in a heap of stones. He crept nearer and saw the white gander laboriously climbing up a cairn of stones with a large bunch of root fibres in his beak. The boy didn't call out, because he thought it would be good to find out first what it was that had made the gander disappear in this way.

A young grey goose cried out with delight when the gander appeared, and the boy crept even closer to see and hear better. The young goose had injured one wing and couldn't fly. Her flock had left her now and she would certainly have died of starvation if the gander hadn't heard her faint cries and carried food to her.

"Goodnight," he said. "I'll come again tomorrow. I won't be leaving for some time and you'll soon be better."

When the gander had gone, the boy crept up among the stones. He was certainly going to tell her that there was no question of Martin staying. But when he saw the grey goose, he understood his friend. She had the most beautiful little head imaginable, her plumage as if of silk and her eyes gentle and pleading.

"Don't be afraid of me," said the boy, when she tried to run away, although her left wing was out of joint and dragging along the ground.

"I'm Tom Thumb, Martin's travelling companion."

When the young goose heard this, she gracefully lowered her head and said in a beautiful soft voice: "Then I'm glad you've come. The white gander has told me

33

that no one is as wise and good as you are."

He felt a great desire to help her, so he thrust his small hands in under her feathers and felt along the wing bone. Nothing was broken, but there was something wrong with the joint. He took a firm hold on the bone and pulled it back into place. The poor young goose let out a shrill cry and sank to the stones as if dead.

The boy was terribly frightened — he had wanted to help her and now she was dead. He ran away. To him, it was if he had killed someone.

The next morning the mists had cleared and Akka decided to move on. The boy was pleased, because his conscience was troubling him. He had said nothing to the gander about what happened when he tried to cure the grey goose. But he wondered whether Martin would have the heart to leave her.

The flock set off and the great white gander reluctantly went with them. But he suddenly turned back, the thought of the young goose overwhelming him. The journey to Lapland would have to look after itself. He couldn't go with the rest of them while she was lying sick and alone, perhaps starving to death.

With a few wingbeats, Martin was there by the pile of stones, but there was no grey goose lying among them.

"Dunfin! Dunfin! Where are you?" called the gander anxiously.

Nils thought perhaps a fox had been and taken her.

But at that moment he heard a beautiful voice answering the gander.

"Here I am, here I am! I was just taking my morning bath." And out of the water came the little grey goose, quite well and in good condition. She told the gander that Tom Thumb had made her wing better and now she was ready to go with them on the journey.

Drops of water lay like splashes of pearls on her silky shimmering feathers, and Tom Thumb thought she looked like a real little princess.

Chapter 7

The wild geese spent the night on the northern tip of Öland and had to struggle against a fierce wind on their way to the mainland. When they reached the first skerries, they heard a great roar and the water beneath them suddenly turned quite black. The geese flew lower, but before they had reached the water, the storm from the west caught up with them and hurled them out towards the open sea. The waves were running high and sea-green with white foam on the crests. The wild geese allowed themselves to be carried up on to the tops of the waves and down into the valleys, having as much fun as children on a seesaw. The poor land birds drifting by in the storm cried out with envy: "Those who can swim have no need to complain."

The wild geese were certainly not out of danger. They grew helplessly sleepy on their seesaws and over and over again, Akka had to call out: "Don't fall asleep! Anyone who falls asleep will lose the flock!"

And yet many of them did. Akka herself was almost asleep when she suddenly saw something round and dark rising above the crest of a wave.

Seals! Seals! Seals!" she called shrilly, and they all rose into the air with a great flapping of wings, the seals so close they snapped at the feet of the last goose.

The storm lasted all day. The geese were deathly tired and to add to everything else, the sea was full of ice floes crashing against each other. They were worried about the night and could still see no land. Darkness fell quickly, the moon hidden behind the clouds, the ice floes crashing and the seals singing their wild hunting songs. It was as if heaven and earth were about to fall apart.

But then the boy thought the roar was suddenly even greater and straight ahead of him at a distance of only few metres he saw a bare rough mountain wall. The geese were flying straight at the cliff, so how could they possibly escape crashing into it?

Then he saw the small opening to a cave — the geese flew straight into it and the next moment they were in safety.

The first thing the travellers thought about was to see if everyone had been saved. None was missing except Kaksi, but she was old and wise and would be sure to find them soon.

They were all delighted with the fine shelter they had found, but suddenly Yksi saw some glimmering green dots in the darkness.

"Those are eyes! There are wild animals in here!" cried Akka in terror, and the geese rushed back towards the entrance. But Nils could see better than the geese, and he called them back.

"That's nothing to be afraid of. They're only kind sheep." The geese greeted the sheep, bobbing up and down, but the leader, a large ram, said not a word in welcome and the sheep just sighed heavily.

"Forgive us for intruding like this," Akka said, "but we were driven by the storm all day and it would be good if we could stay here where it's safe."

Again there was a great sighing inside the cave and one ewe said: "It's not at all safe here. You'd be better off flying around in the storm than staying here. But you mustn't leave before we may offer you something to eat," and she indicated a pool of water and a pile of chaff and husks. That was a feast and the geese threw themselves on to the food.

After they had eaten, all they wanted to do was to sleep. But then the great ram rose and said: "This is Lilla Karlsö island off Gotland. No one lives here except sheep and sea birds. We look after ourselves and live in caves all the year round. The grazing is good up here on the mountain. But last winter, it was so cold the straits froze over and three foxes came across the ice from the mainland. They creep up on us when we're asleep and they have savaged and killed nearly all of us. We here in the cave are the only ones left, and soon we won't be able to keep watch any more." The ram sighed heavily.

Akka was reluctant to take the flock back into the storm. She turned to Nils and asked him to stand guard outside the cave and warn them if the foxes appeared, so that they could fly away.

He was only moderately pleased with the assignment, but anything was better than going back into that storm. He sat down in the lee behind a stone but soon saw three foxes creeping up the slope. Thinking it would a great pity to wake the geese and leave the sheep to their fate, he nipped back inside, tugged at the ram's horn and swung up on his back.

"Up you get, Father. We're going to scare off those foxes!" The foxes had stopped in the cave entrance at first, but now they were sneaking further in.

"Charge straight ahead!" the boy whispered in the ram's ear. The great ram charged and the first fox was thrown head over heels out of the cave.

"Charge to the left!" cried the boy, steering the ram's head in that direction. The ram aimed a tremendous blow at the second fox and rammed it in its side. It tumbled over and over before fleeing, the third fox hard at its heels.

"I think they've had enough for tonight," said the boy.

"I'm sure they have," said the ram. "Now you lie down in the wool on my back and go to sleep."

The next day, the ram went around with the boy on his back to show him the island, which was like a large round house with perpendicular walls and a flat roof.

"If you're on your own, you must watch out for cracks in the roof. If you fall down one, that's the end of you!" the ram warned him. The cliffs were full of birds' nests, though today eider ducks, guillemots and razorbills were all out on the sunlit sea, fishing for herring.

The remains of the foxes' meals were strewn all along the shore. Nils was horrified and miserable and would really have liked to help the sheep if only he could find a way.

Later that day, the gander took the boy on his back and wandered around on the roof of the mountain. He was limping and dragging one wing while the boy lay looking up into the blue sky, so neither of them noticed that the three foxes had come up on to the mountain. When the foxes saw that Martin couldn't fly away, they at once made for him. Poor Martin fled as fast as he could, while the boy teasingly shouted: "Have you eaten so much mutton that you can't even catch a goose!"

That made the foxes mad with rage and they prepared for one last leap. But the gander rushed straight towards the deepest ravine, then he flapped once with his wings and managed to get across.

"Stop now, Martin," said the boy after the gander had run a little way on the other side. Behind them they could hear wild howls and the thuds of heavy falls. But they saw no more of the foxes.

That night the geese slept out on the mountain and the boy lay in the short dry grass. The moon was full and round, so it was hard to sleep. He reckoned it must be the night before Easter Sunday.

As he lay there thinking, he saw a bird outlined in black against the moon, and a moment later a handsome stork was beside him asking him if he would like to go on a flying trip in the beautiful moonlight. They had once met at Glimmingehus and Nils was pleased to see him again. So off they went, heading straight towards the moon, but after a while the stork landed on a deserted sea shore of fine level sand. He drew up one leg and said: "I'll take a little rest here. Meanwhile you can take a look round, but don't go too far."

Nils thought he might go up on to a sand dune and see what the land looked like on the other side. Then his clog struck something hard and there in the sand lay a thin verdigris green copper coin, so worn he didn't bother to pick it up. But when he raised his eyes again, he was amazed – two steps away was a dark high wall with a great towered portal, the glittering sea quite hidden by the wall. The boy realized there was something ghostly about this, but he very much wanted to know what was behind the portal, so he quickly went in.

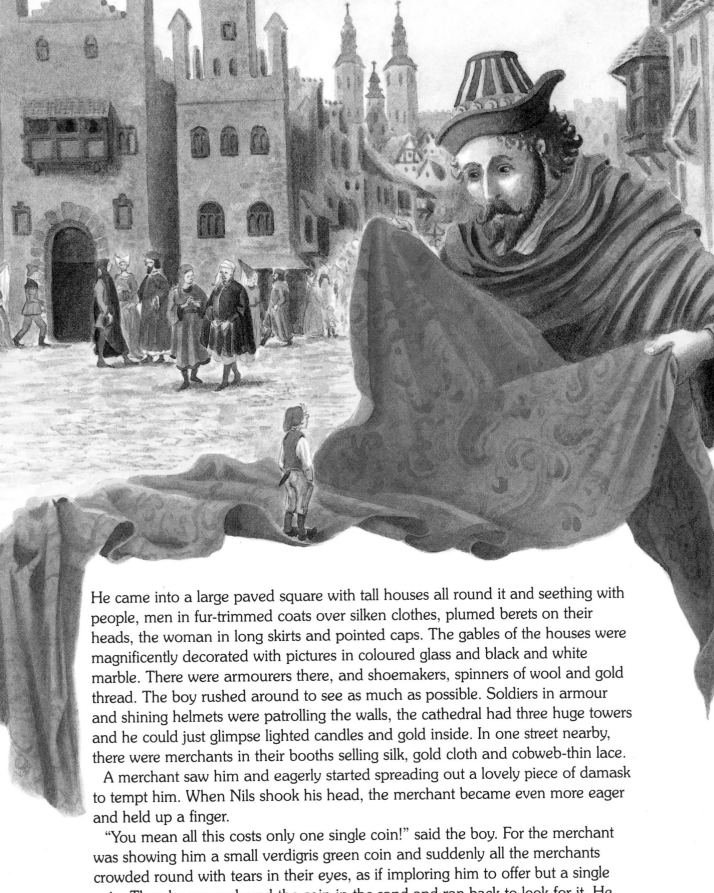

He came into a large paved square with tall houses all round it and seething with
people, men in fur-trimmed coats over silken clothes, plumed berets on their
heads, the woman in long skirts and pointed caps. The gables of the houses were
magnificently decorated with pictures in coloured glass and black and white
marble. There were armourers there, and shoemakers, spinners of wool and gold
thread. The boy rushed around to see as much as possible. Soldiers in armour
and shining helmets were patrolling the walls, the cathedral had three huge towers
and he could just glimpse lighted candles and gold inside. In one street nearby,
there were merchants in their booths selling silk, gold cloth and cobweb-thin lace.

A merchant saw him and eagerly started spreading out a lovely piece of damask
to tempt him. When Nils shook his head, the merchant became even more eager
and held up a finger.

"You mean all this costs only one single coin!" said the boy. For the merchant
was showing him a small verdigris green coin and suddenly all the merchants
crowded round with tears in their eyes, as if imploring him to offer but a single
coin. Then he remembered the coin in the sand and ran back to look for it. He
found it and was about to hurry back, but then the town had vanished and all he
could see in front of him was the sea.

He felt the stork nudging him with his beak. "You seem to be standing there fast asleep, like me," he said.

"What was that town I saw?" said the boy.

"You were probably dreaming," said the stork. "But I have to tell you that they say there was once long ago a magnificent town here called Vineta. As punishment for the arrogance of the inhabitants, it was sent to the bottom of the sea. For one hour only every hundred years, it is allowed to come up again in all its glory. If a merchant had succeeded in selling you something, Tom Thumb, then the town would have been allowed to stay on land and its people live and die like the rest of us."

"Then that was the town I saw," said Nils. "You brought me here so that I could save it. And then I didn't ..."

He put his face in his hands and wept. For two days, the boy was quite unlike himself, speaking not a single happy word, and grieving that he had not been able to save that wonderful town. Akka and the gander both told him it had been a dream or an optical illusion, but the boy didn't want to believe them and was profoundly distressed.

At that moment, Kaksi returned to the flock, and she certainly knew what to do.

"If Tom Thumb is grieving for an old town, we can soon console him. Just you come with me."

The wild geese said goodbye to the sheep and flew to Gotland. Nils sat there looking down at the flat island with its budding trees and flowering meadows. Without him noticing, the geese flew west towards the coast, but then he happened to raise his eyes and his astonishment was beyond all words. The blue sea lay before him, on the shore a town with walls and towers, churches and gabled houses quite black against the bright sky. They looked just as handsome as those he had seen on Easter Eve. But he soon realized there was just as great a difference between the two as when one day you see a man in purple silk and jewels, and the next day poor and in rags. In the town of Visby, which had been allowed to stay on land, the tall church towers were roofless, the windows gaping and empty, the floors overgrown with grass, the glittering glory all gone.

Who knows whether the sunken town had not become as decayed as this one, thought Nils. Perhaps it was just as well things had gone as they had. Then he stopped grieving over it all but nonetheless gave no thought to the town being beautiful with its creeper-covered ruins and gardens full of fragrant roses. Many people take more delight in the Visby that exists than in the magnificent Vineta on the seabed.

Chapter 8

The wild geese had had a good journey across the sea and had landed in north Småland, an area which didn't seem to be able to decide whether it wanted to be land or sea — bays curving in and out everywhere, dividing the coast into islands and peninsulas, headlands and isthmuses. Spring had made great progress while they had been out on the island. Although the splendid big trees were not yet out, the ground beneath them was bright with blue hepaticas, yellow stars of Bethlehem and wood anemones. When the wild geese saw this carpet of flowers, they feared they had stayed too long in the south, so next morning Akka set course directly to the bare top of Taberg where they used to rest every year.

The first people to see the geese that lovely spring morning were the mine-workers at Taberg breaking up iron ore on the surface of the mountain. A driller stopped drilling holes in the rock for a while and called out happily: "Where are you off to?"

The geese didn't understand what he had said, but the boy shouted as loudly as he could: "To where there are neither pickaxes nor hammers!" The driller stared up in surprise — he thought it must be his own longing that meant that he could understand the geese's cackling call so well.

Up on the mountain, the boy could see very far all round, in the east, south and west nothing but poor high land with dark pine forests and ice-covered lakes. But to the north, he could see only soft valleys and winding rivers, right up to the great Lake Vätter. The lake was free of ice and shone as if it were filled with blue light instead of water.

When the geese then went on, they came over the match factories of Jönköping and the women workers filling matchboxes inside them.

"Where are you going?" one of them called, leaning out of the window. And the boy replied happily: "Where there's no need for matches or candles."

In the school yard in Huskvarna, the children stood in a line and called out: "Where are you going?"

"Where there's no school or lessons!" the boy yelled in reply.

The journey continued over the great bird lake Tåkern, over Vadstena and the convent of St Birgitta and out over the plain of Östgöta. The boy counted the many white churches protruding up out of clumps of trees, and he got to fifty before he gave up. He thought the farms and palaces, towns and factories and railway stations were scattered over the lovely plain like pearls set round a priceless jewel.

Along the Göta canal, they were preparing for spring, men mending the canal banks and tarring the great lock gates. Everywhere, in the towns as well, they were cleaning and sweeping up to receive the spring. In Norrköping, there were masons and painters on scaffolding outside the houses and women were cleaning the windows, while down in the harbour the sailing boats and steamers were all being made shipshape.

But then the time had come to leave the plains and take the route over Kolmården, the great forest that lay there so dark, thick and wild. They rested by a forest lake and the next day went on north over Sörmland. The boy looked down at the landscape and thought it was unlike any he had seen previously. Here they had taken a great lake and a great river and a great forest and a great mountain and hacked them to pieces and mixed them up and flung them out in any old order, he thought, for he could see nothing but small valleys and small hills and small clumps of woodland. Everywhere there were proud trees, lovely flowers and the water in the little canals was clear and a glimmering dark green. Nils thought it all looked like paradise.

"I've never seen anything so beautiful. What kind of garden is that?"

In one bay in a lake, on a headland almost completely surrounded by water, he saw the largest and most splendid castle of all, its mighty round towers rising high above the treetops. The geese landed there to graze and Nils ran inquisitively up to the palace to take a closer look at it.

He walked through the deep archway and came into a large triangular courtyard, where there were two long cannons. He had to leapfrog over them before he ran on into yet another courtyard. He went inside and came to a row of large old-world halls, their walls covered with tall dark pictures of solemn gentlemen and ladies in peculiar stiff costumes. He also found a little theatre, and quite near to it a real prison, a room with bare walls and barred windows, the floor worn down by the feet of prisoners.

"Did you see King Erik, who was imprisoned in Gripsholm Castle?" asked Akka when Nils came back.

They had come a good way across Sörmland when the boy saw something dark moving along the ground beneath them. At first he thought it was a dog, and would not have given it another thought if it hadn't been that it was keeping the same course as the geese. It was dashing across open fences, through clumps of woodland and over ditches without stopping. It looks almost like Smirre the fox, he thought — and at that moment, the geese set off at tremendous speed, turned and took a wide sweep to the west.

"It must have been Smirre the fox," the boy said to himself. "That's why Akka is taking another route."

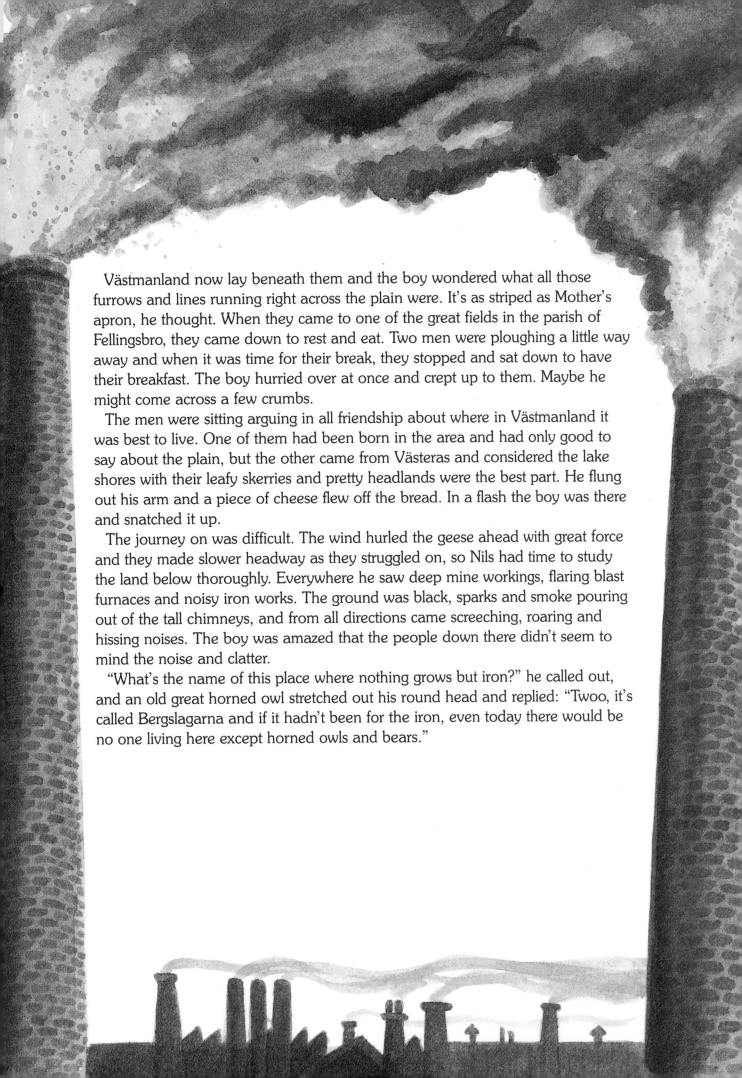

Västmanland now lay beneath them and the boy wondered what all those furrows and lines running right across the plain were. It's as striped as Mother's apron, he thought. When they came to one of the great fields in the parish of Fellingsbro, they came down to rest and eat. Two men were ploughing a little way away and when it was time for their break, they stopped and sat down to have their breakfast. The boy hurried over at once and crept up to them. Maybe he might come across a few crumbs.

The men were sitting arguing in all friendship about where in Västmanland it was best to live. One of them had been born in the area and had only good to say about the plain, but the other came from Västeras and considered the lake shores with their leafy skerries and pretty headlands were the best part. He flung out his arm and a piece of cheese flew off the bread. In a flash the boy was there and snatched it up.

The journey on was difficult. The wind hurled the geese ahead with great force and they made slower headway as they struggled on, so Nils had time to study the land below thoroughly. Everywhere he saw deep mine workings, flaring blast furnaces and noisy iron works. The ground was black, sparks and smoke pouring out of the tall chimneys, and from all directions came screeching, roaring and hissing noises. The boy was amazed that the people down there didn't seem to mind the noise and clatter.

"What's the name of this place where nothing grows but iron?" he called out, and an old great horned owl stretched out his round head and replied: "Twoo, it's called Bergslagarna and if it hadn't been for the iron, even today there would be no one living here except horned owls and bears."

After that, the flight of the wild geese ran into southern Dalarna, and mines, iron workings and iron works continued below them. But when they arrived at the River Dal, Nils had something else to look at. This was the first really big river he had come across and he was amazed when he saw the great mass of water gliding through the countryside. He saw the great waterfalls at Domnarvet and Kvarnsveden and the great works they were to drive. He saw the floating bridges on the river, the ferries it bore, the logs it rolled forward, the railway following it, then crossing it, and it dawned on him what a great and remarkable water course it was.

All through the afternoon, the wild geese flew back and forth across the great Lake Silja to find a place to land. They showed the boy the big churches and villages round the lake, the villages like small towns, and Nils was surprised how built up it was here in the north.

Darkness fell and the geese settled down to sleep on the ice on Lake Silja, the wind so cold, the boy crept in under the gander's wing, only to be woken shortly afterwards by the sound of gunshots. He tumbled out and looked round in terror. Great bonfires were burning all along the curve of the shore and up on the hills, shot after shot ringing out and rockets soaring up into the sky.

"It's human children playing," said Akka, and went back to sleep.

Like a mosquito, the boy was attracted by the light and warmth, so he ran over to the mainland. Very cautiously, he slipped up to a bonfire on the actual bank of the lake, where there were people in the prettiest costumes Nils had ever seen. He sat there for a long time, listening to them laughing and talking, and to the songs they were singing out into the night.

When he finally ran back in the darkness to his travelling companions, the sounds of the singing and music were still ringing in his ears.

Next morning, the sun was shining, but there was still snow on the ground, so to find food, the geese had to fly back to the southeast. It was Sunday and the church bells could be heard ringing everywhere for morning service, the still air as if changed out of all recognition by the notes. One thing was certain, thought the boy, and that is wherever I go in this country I'll hear bells ringing. The thought made him feel safe. He would never get lost as long as the ringing of bells could call to him.

Chapter 9

For several days, the weather was terrible, the wind howling and the rain slashing down. Both people and animals knew this was inevitable for spring to arrive, but all the same they found it almost unbearable.

The snow was now melting fast, water dripping and rustling and rippling everywhere. The spring streams started and in many places floods were threatening the dwellings of both animals and people.

The wild geese struggled against the west wind as best they could, but nonetheless they were thrown off course, and before the wind dropped and the sun peeped out, they had been driven back to the shores of Lake Mälare.

The boy noticed the water in the lake was rising for every minute, the level up the trunks of the willows and elders along the shores already high, and the lovely shore walk had become a rushing stream. In Köping people were rowing boats along the streets, and he saw two elks swimming ashore from a small skerry.

In Hjälstaviken, the swan's nests had been torn from their moorings and were drifting away in the strong wind. Some had already fallen apart and he could see eggs glinting on the lake bed. Hundreds of wild swans, white and shimmering, were swimming round in the bay.

The wild geese had found a place to sleep a little further out in Ekolsund. But Nils was far too hungry to be able to sleep. I must try to get into some cottage or other to find some food, he thought.

As so many things were floating round in the water, it wasn't difficult to find a craft which would do for someone like Nils. He jumped on to a piece of planking, fished out a little stick and poled his way towards the shore. He had scarcely landed when he heard a splashing in the water. A female swan was sleeping on her nest only a few metres away. He kept quite still and suddenly found a four-legged scoundrel had already taken a few steps out into the water and was about to creep up on the swan's nest.

"Hey, hey!" yelled the boy at the top of his voice, slapping the water with his stick. The swan rose, but had he wanted to, the fox could easily have caught her.

Instead, the fox headed straight for the boy, who ran off inland, where there were large fields but not a tree in sight to climb up, nor a hole to hide in. It was true he was a good runner, but it was also obvious he couldn't compete with a fox that was free and had nothing to carry.

There were lights on in the windows of some cottages a little way away from the shore, so he ran towards them. A dog was barking and by the nearest cottage a large handsome guard dog was standing outside his kennel.

"Listen, guard dog, would you help me catch a fox tonight?" the boy said quietly. The guard dog couldn't see very well and he was also angry about being chained up.

"Making a fool of me, are you?" he barked. "You just come within reach, and I'll teach you a thing or two. No one plays the fool with me."

"I'm not frightened," said the boy, running up to the dog, who was so surprised, he fell quiet. "I'm Tom Thumb and I'm travelling round with the wild geese. Maybe you've heard about me?"

"Yes, the sparrows have indeed twittered a little," the dog replied. "They say you've done great things, although you're so small."

"Well, things have been more or less all right so far," said the boy. "But it looks as it won't be all that good for me if you don't help me. I've a fox at my heels. He's hiding round the corner there."

"Yes, I can smell him all right, but we'll soon get rid of him," said the dog, barking as loudly as he could.

"You'll need more than a fine bark to frighten that fox," said the boy. "I know how we could catch him, you and I."

The boy and the guard dog crept into the kennel and lay there whispering to each other.

After a while, they saw the fox sticking its nose round the corner of the cottage, then sitting down at distance, speculating on how he could lure Nils Gooseboy out. The guard dog in his turn stuck his head out and growled: "Go away, or I'll get you!"

"I'll sit here as long as I want to," replied the fox.

"Go away!" snarled the dog threateningly. "Otherwise you've gone hunting for the very last time."

"I know how long your chain is," scoffed the fox, not budging an inch.

"Then you've only yourself to blame," said the dog, and he took a great leap at the fox and caught him without any difficulty, for the boy had undone his collar and let him loose. The battle was soon over, the dog the victor and the fox lying on the ground, not daring to move.

"Yes, you just keep still," said the dog. "Otherwise I'll bite you to death." He took the fox by the scruff of the neck and dragged him over to the kennel. The boy brought out the chain, wound the collar twice round the fox's neck, then fastened it.

"Well, I hope you'll make a good guard dog, Smirre Fox," said the boy when he had finished.

Chapter 10

The weather had suddenly turned fine, warm, calm and pleasant. Nils Holgersson was lying on a clump of marsh marigolds enjoying the sun when a raven came flying down and settled among the bright flowers. It was Bataki. The boy had had dealings with him before and knew that he couldn't always be relied on. Bataki was looking dismal and solemn, but nonetheless the boy thought he could see a mischievous glint in his eye. The raven had surely come to make a fool of him, so Nils decided to take no notice of what he said.

"That was clever of you to catch Smirre the fox," said the raven, "so I'll tell you a secret. You see, I can tell you what to do to become human again."

Bataki probably thought Nils would at once snap up the bait, but the boy simply said he already knew. As long as he got the white gander safely back home to Skåne, then ...

But if it goes wrong, perhaps you'll need another way out," said Bataki. "Though I don't have to tell you."

"Tell me your secret then."

"I'll tell you when the right moment comes. Get on my back and come with me, and we'll see what happens."

The boy hesitated, because he never quite knew where he was with the raven.

"Oh, so you don't dare," croaked Bataki. Nils couldn't bear those words, so a moment later he was up on the raven's back. They set off, and in next to no time were in Uppasala and Bataki came down on a roof.

"Look around and tell me who you think rules things in this town," he said.

"It might be the King," said Nils, who had seen a handsome castle with two mighty towers.

"Not a bad guess," replied the raven. "But that was in the old days."

The cathedral and its tall spires and handsome portals were gleaming in the evening sun.

"Perhaps the bishop and his priests?" the boy suggested.

"Not bad, either, because the Archbishop lives here, but he's not the one who rules here, either."

"Then I don't know," said the boy.

"Well, Academe rules in this town," Bataki informed him. "All those grand buildings you see, they have been put up for him and his people. Come and I'll show you."

The raven took the boy to the university and the library, floating past the windows of research rooms and institutes of all kinds. Everywhere they went, people were reading and studying.

"If I weren't a raven, but just human like you, then I'd settle here and learn everything that is in books," said the raven. "Wouldn't you like to do that, too?"

"Oh, no," said Nils. "I'd rather go around with the wild geese."

"Don't you want to be someone who cures illnesses, or knows everything about the sun and moon, or speaks all languages?"

Well, that might be quite fun.

"Or someone who knows the difference between right and wrong, good and evil. Then you could preach in church back home ..."

A glimmer came into the boy's eyes.

"Father and Mother would be pleased if I got that far," he said.

A great crowd of young people wearing white caps had assembled in the Botanical Gardens and were singing spring songs, making speeches and cheering. Their cheerfulness was such that the boy suddenly felt how deplorable his own life was, almost so much so, he almost lost his desire to return to his travelling companions.

Then the raven started croaking again.

"I'll tell you that secret now, Tom Thumb," he said. "You must wait until you meet someone who tells you he would like to be in your shoes and travel round with the wild geese. Then you must say this ..." Bataki whispered a few words in his ear, words that were so powerful and dangerous, they couldn't be said out aloud if you seriously wished to use them.

"Well, I don't suppose that will ever come about," said the boy. "Help me instead to find a little food, I'm so terribly hungry."

The raven took a turn across the town and put Nils down on the roof outside an attic room. Inside, the lamp was on although the student who lived in the room was asleep in bed. The window was slightly open and a half-eaten sandwich was lying on the table. The boy was soon feasting on it, smacking his lips at every mouthful.

"Hullo there, and who might you be?" said a voice. Nils jumped, but the student was sitting up in bed and he looked kind.

"My name's Nils Holgersson, and I'm human though I've been turned into a gnome. And now I'm travelling round with the wild geese," he replied brightly.

"How very strange," said the student. Then he asked Nils about everything that had happened and in the end he said:

"Oh, if only I were in your shoes and could leave behind all my troubles!" Bataki tapped on the window with his beak and the boy's head whirled, his heart thumping; they sounded almost like the right words ...

"Surely you don't want to change with me? Surely a student doesn't want to be anything else?"

"Oh, you should know what happened to me today," sighed the student. Then he told Nils that that very morning a timid and poor friend had come to see him, bearing with him a thick bundle, a manuscript he had been working on for five years, and now he wanted to hear the student's honest opinion of it. The student had been just about to leave for his final exam, but nevertheless sat down and started reading at once, page after page.

"When this book is published, his happiness will be complete," he said to himself. "It will be fun to tell him that." But at that moment he looked at the time and seeing that he was late, he hurried out through the door. In the draught, the window blew open and all the papers on the table swirled out over the rooftops.

In despair, the student rushed back in and tried to rescue some of the pages. But he simply had to hurry off to his exam. It will affect my whole future, he thought and dashed away. But he was so upset everything he had learnt also seemed to have been blown away, and he failed to do very well. When he got back to his room, he looked out on to the roof to see if there were any pages there, but not a single one was left. How would he be able to tell his friend the book was a masterpiece but the manuscript was lost. No one would believe him ...

"I can't bear the thought of making a friend so unhappy," groaned the student. "It'd be much better for me if I were in your shoes and could go off with the wild geese."

Again Bataki tapped hard on the window, but the boy sat there in silence for a long time. "Wait a moment," he said in a low voice, then slowly stepped out on to the windowsill, and at that moment the sun rose and shone and glistened on all the temples and towers of this town of learning.

"What do you think you're doing?" said the raven. "Now you've lost your chance of being human."

"I'm not going to change," said Nils. "I would only have all those miseries over the lost papers."

"I can probably get them back," said Bataki.

"I'm sure you can, but I first want to see you do it," said Nils.

The raven flew off and came back with two pages. For a whole hour, he flew back and forth with more and more pages in his beak.

"I think they're all here now," he gasped, but then he saw the student already putting the papers in order.

"You're the silliest donkey I've ever come across!" the raven shrieked at Nils. "Have you given him the book? Now he'll never say he wished he was in your shoes."

The boy was also looking at the happy student.

"Thank you, Bataki," he said. "I realize you were testing me out. I suppose you thought I would let Martin look after himself on this difficult journey as soon as things turned out well for me. But when this student told me his story, I thought about how horrible it was to betray a friend, so I didn't want to do that, either."

Bataki scratched the back of his head and looked embarrassed, then flew straight over the cathedral back to the geese.

Chapter 11

Dunfin already knew where she was by Lake Mälare, for her parents lived on a skerry further out, on the edge of the archipelago, and now she kindly invited the wild geese to her home so that she could show her family she was alive. No one could be gentler than the little grey goose.

"When she asks for something, not even Akka can say no," said Martin. And it would only delay their journey by one day.

They set off and flew east across Lake Mälare. The further east they went, the more lively the lake became and the more buildings there were on the shores. The boy was looking down on all the strange little villas when Dunfinlet out a cry: "There's the town that swims on the water. Now I know where I am!" At first Nils could see nothing but mists, but here and there a tall spire protruding, but when he got closer, the mists rose and he could just see roofs and gables and houses with rows and rows of windows, he realized he was above a large town. It looked almost enchanted in the swirling mist coloured by the light of the morning sun.

When the geese came to Dunfin's island, her parents were delighted to find their daughter in this crowd of strange birds. The wild geese were so well received, they decided to stay there overnight.

The next morning the boy was still asleep among the geese when he heard Dunfin calling: "Tom Thumb, Tom Thumb! Martin's being attacked by an eagle." Like lightning, Nils leapt up on to Dunfin's back and they found Martin battling away with a golden eagle, bleeding and ruffled, but still fighting bravely. The boy realized he could do nothing himself and that help was needed.

"Quick, Dunfin. Call up Akka and the wild geese!"

The eagle at once stopped and let Martin go.

"Greetings to Akka from Gorgo the eagle and tell her I never expected to meet her or her flock out here on the edge of the archipelago," he said, then swerved swiftly away. Nils could only stare after him in bewilderment.

Akka wouldn't explain who Gorgo was. She called the flock together and they were soon all on their way over the little island. Then suddenly a gull swooped down on the big white gander, grabbed the boy and flew away with him in its beak. There was a wild chase over the islands, and in their fervour, the geese didn't notice they were above a boat where a fisherman was sitting with a gun in his hand. He fired a shot and at that moment the gull opened its beak and dropped the boy into the sea.

Nils Holgersson was lying at the bottom of a basket, bound hand and foot, the lid firmly closed. He was quite worried because he didn't know what was going to happen. All he knew was that the fisherman was taking him somewhere.

The fisherman suddenly stopped and asked someone whether the supervisor was at home. "I think so," said an old man's voice. "What've you got today, then? A fine live sea bird as usual?"

"See for yourself and tell me what I can ask for this joker," said the fisherman, opening the lid. The boy looked up in terror at a bearded old face.

"What on earth — how did you get hold of that?" said the old man, starting back.

"Are you afraid of him?" laughed the fisherman, closing the lid and putting the basket down on the ground. "He came all by himself, straight out of the sky. I took my gun with me when I went fishing this morning, and I'd hardly set out before I saw some wild geese and fired off a shot. I didn't hit anything, but instead this creature came tumbling down and all I had to do was to fish him out with the net."

"Surely you didn't shoot him?" said the old man anxiously.

"No, he's all right. But he was rather stunned at first, so I took the opportunity to tie him up so he shouldn't escape. I at once thought Dr Hazelius here at Skansen might like him."

The boy had heard about Skansen, where everything old and good from all over the country had been assembled: peasant's cottages, manor houses, charcoal burners's cabins and clock towers, household goods and national costumes of all kinds. You could look at wild as well as tame animals there, too, elks and bears, seals and deer, horses, cows and sheep, monkeys and peacocks.

So perhaps he would be put in a pen now and exhibited, be given a doll's house to live in, and people would come and look at him as if he were a monster? The boy turned over and through a hole near the bottom of the basket found himself looking straight at a squirrel clinging to a tree-trunk.

That gave him courage. He managed to get out his sheath-knife and started sawing away at the string.

"Didn't he say anything?" said the old man.

"Yes, he called to the geese and they called back to him. They followed me all the way home, making a terrible fuss. But then I put one of the children's dolls in the window, and the geese thought it was him, so I could go off with my basket in peace. How much do you think the doctor would give me for him?"

Nils heard no more, because he had managed to crawl out of the basket, then slip into the bushes to hide.

It wasn't difficult to while away the time at Skansen. He made the acquaintance of all the animals and found many friends. As he had often been very cold in the bad weather on his way, he thought it would a good idea to break off his journey. Perhaps he would have simply frozen to death by now if he had got to Lapland. Anyhow, he had no choice but to stay, though he very much missed Martin and the others.

The days grew warmer and summer really came, the ground green, the silky green leaves out on the birches and poplars, the cherry trees in full bloom and tiny unripe fruit already on the currant bushes. I suppose it's lovely and warm up in Lapland now, too, he thought miserably.

Then one day the boy happened to walk past the outdoor eagle cage made of iron poles and wire, so big there was room for several trees inside and also a cairn of stones to make the eagles feel at home. Yet they didn't like it. They perched on the same spot nearly all day, without moving, their lovely dark plumage ruffled and dull, their eyes staring with hopeless yearning into space.

Nils heard a keeper saying that one of the eagles was a newcomer and had been there no longer than a week at the most. The new one was just as immobile, but his plumage was still shiny and beautiful — then suddenly the boy knew who it was.

"Gorgo! Gorgo!" he called from down on the ground. The eagle was so drowsy he could hardly lower his eyes.

"Who is that calling me?" he asked feebly.

"Gorgo! It's Tom Thumb, who flies with the wild geese. Don't you remember me?"

"Have they caught Akka, too?" the eagle asked, as if trying to collect his wits after a long sleep.

"No, all the others are probably fit and well up in Lapland by now. I'm the only one who has ended up here. Can I help you in any way, Gorgo?"

"Don't disturb me, Tom Thumb. I sit here dreaming I'm hovering freely around in space. I don't want to be awake."

"No, Golden Eagle, you must move and take note of what's going on. Otherwise you'll become as miserable as the others."

"I wish I was like them," said the eagle. "Nothing can disturb them any longer."

The boy walked thoughtfully away.

When night came, a faint scraping noise could be heard on the roof of the eagle's cage. Gorgo woke and raised his head to see the boy clinging to the wire and filing away. "I'm a big bird, Tom Thumb," said the eagle. "How can you file through so many wires so that I can get out? You might as well stop."

"You just go to sleep," said the boy. "Don't bother about me. I'm going to try to let you out, because you'll only be completely destroyed here."

The next day the eagle saw that several wires had been cut through and he at once felt less drowsy. He hopped about on the branches of the tree and flapped his wings to get the stiffness out of his body.

Early one morning, just as the first strip of light appeared in the sky, Tom Thumb woke the eagle. "Try now, Gorgo!"

The eagle looked up. There was a large hole in the roof and the eagle threw himself at it, missed a couple of times, but then he was safely out and away, rising in proud flight and disappearing.

Nils stayed where he was gazing after the eagle. Oh, if only I could go with him, he thought sadly. Just imagine riding on the gander's back and seeing Akka again ...

Suddenly the eagle swooped down out of a cloud and perched beside him on the roof of the cage.

"I wanted to try out my wings to see if they still worked," said Gorgo. "You didn't think I'd leave you behind in captivity, did you?" At that he scooped up Nils Holgersson with his great foot, rose with him up into the sky, and soon they were racing away to the north.

Chapter 12

The eagle and the boy flew right up through Uppland without stopping until they came to Älvekarleby, where the eagle came down on a stone in the middle of the river, just below a rushing waterfall, the white wall of foam from the waterfall above them and the river racing all round them.

"I'll tell you now why I want to take you back to the wild geese," said Gorgo. Then he told Nils about the big eagle eyrie up on the cliff edge high above a hidden valley. Far down below gleamed the small lake, and on its tussocky shore, the wild geese were nesting and hatching their young among dwarf birches and osiers. The eagles never took more geese than they needed, so the geese continue to breed in the valley, for they also benefited from one lot of robbers keeping others away.

But then one evening, the leader goose noticed the parent eagles did not return to the eyrie, and in the stillness of the morning, they heard pitiful cries coming from up above. The leader goose flew up high to be able to look down into the eyrie and there, among whitening bones, blood-stained feathers and hare's feet, lay a semi-naked eaglet, screaming.

"Was that you? And Akka?" said the boy.

"Yes, it was. I don't remember myself, but Akka has often told me about it. Let me go on now."

The eaglet was a proper rascal. "Go and get me some food at once!" he screamed. "It's shameful of mother to let me starve. What are you sitting there staring at? Are you deaf? I need food!"

The wild goose presumed the parent birds had been shot, and if she let the eaglet starve, the geese would be left in peace. But it wasn't in her nature to refuse to help a deserted creature. So she flew away and was soon back with a char she had just caught. Instead of thanking her, the eaglet struck fiercely out at her. "Do you think I can eat that stuff? I want grouse. Or lemming. And don't you forget it!"

Akka stretched out her neck and nipped him in the skin on the back of his head.

"You'll just have to put up with what I bring," she said. "Your mother and father have gone, but if you wish to starve to death while waiting up here for grouse and lemmings, then that's all right by me." Then she flew away and when she came back, the fish had slipped down into the eaglet's empty stomach. It was hard work finding food for this greedy youngster, who soon came to regard Akka as his real mother.

A week or two later, Akka saw it was moulting-time, when she wouldn't be able to fly.

"I can't fly up with any more food now," she said. "You'll have to pluck up courage and throw yourself down into the valley, where I can feed you as before."

Without a second's hesitation, the eaglet hurtled straight out into the air. He tumbled about for a while but soon got his wings working and came down unhurt. All that summer, he lived with the wild geese and made friends with the goslings. He wanted to live like them, and when they swam out on the lake, he went after them and nearly drowned. But one day he realized he was an eagle after all, and so had to live like an eagle. Akka was proud of having brought him up to be gentle and harmless and was not going to tolerate his desire to live in his own way.

"Do you think I want to be friends with a bird-eater?" she hissed. "You live in the way I have taught you, then you can home with us as before."

But they were both equally proud, and neither would give way.

"So Akka told me never to show myself in her presence again," said Gorgo finally. "And no one may talk to her about me." Then he added: "But I've never attacked a wild goose."

The eagle and the boy flew on over Gästrikland. A plain almost completely covered with spruce forest lay below to the south, and after that came a beautiful area of wooded hills, rushing streams and gleaming lakes. There were thickly populated parishes, and roads and railways crossing each other, and one iron works after another along the water courses, just like the ones the boy had seen in Bergslagarna.

Further north were again dark forests, but now the land ran in mountains and valleys like a rough sea. This landscape wears spruce skirts and grey stone jerseys, thought the boy. And round its waist is a belt embroidered with blue lakes and flowering pastures, the iron works decorating it like a row of jewels, and as a buckle it has a whole town with castle and churches and clusters of houses.

Gorgo eventually came down on a bare mountain slope. "There's game here in the forest and I must go hunting," he said. "You won't be frightened, will you, if I leave for a while?"

"Oh, no, I don't suppose so," said Nils, though he did feel somewhat deserted as he sat down on a stone and looked around.

There had obviously been a forest fire there, for all the trees and plants on the ground had gone, leaving nothing but black stumps between the smooth stones. And after the fire, the wind had swirled away a lot of the good topsoil, leaving the ground dry and loose like ash. The boy thought it all looked dreadful and he couldn't even find a whortleberry to eat.

Then he heard singing down in the forest and saw a procession of people on their way up the ridge, a whole crowd of children with mattocks, spades and packs of food. All the children in the parish had come to plant trees, their teacher with them, followed by the foresters with a load of pine seedlings and spruce seeds. There was life and movement everywhere.

The children started hacking and digging, then planting seedling after seedling on every bare patch of earth they could find. The seedlings were to bind together the remaining soil and then new soil would form between the trees and the seeds would fall into that. So in a few years' time the children would be able to pick raspberries and bilberries, and the seedlings would eventually become great trees. A lot of people came up the hill to watch, but then they also joined in, so it was even more fun.

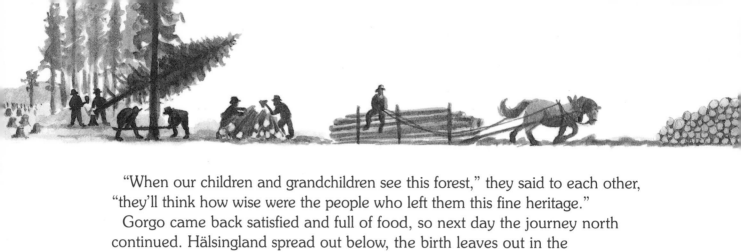

"When our children and grandchildren see this forest," they said to each other, "they'll think how wise were the people who left them this fine heritage."

Gorgo came back satisfied and full of food, so next day the journey north continued. Hälsingland spread out below, the birth leaves out in the pasturelands, the fields green with new grass and young spring corn. It was high mountainous country, but a wide valley ran right through it and everywhere he saw people and cattle leaving the farms and heading for the desolate forest, filling it with life. It seemed to be the custom for farmers to send their cattle to the outfield pastures all on the same day, or perhaps that was what it seemed like this year. All day they could hear the farm girls singing, cattle bellowing and bells jangling as they laboriously made their way along winding paths and across wet mosses deep into the forest. There the land had been cleared for the outfield buildings and small grey cottages and rich lush grass grew all round them. When the cattle got there, they bellowed cheerfully and at once started grazing. The men chopped wood and fetched water, so soon smoke was curling out of chimneys on all the hills round about, while the farm girls set about the first milking.

But when Gorgo was above Medelpad, they could see nothing but dark forests and the boy sighed. "No people could possibly live here."

"They have the forest as their fields," said the eagle.

"Anyone trying to make a living out of fields like that would need a lot of patience," said Nils. "The rye fields at home grow during one summer, but the forests need years to ripen into a harvest."

Next Gorgo wanted to show him how farming the forest was done, so he took the route over an area of bare stumps and cleared undergrowth.

"That's a field that was mown last winter," he said.

"In Skåne," said Nils, "we gather in the harvest in a few days, but this must take several weeks. They must be clever people to be able to mow a field like that."

A little further on they saw a wretched road that was narrow and crooked, stony and uneven.

"The crop is hauled down that road to the stack," said the eagle. Then they came to a river bank covered with sawdust and bark.

"That's where the crop has been stacked," said Gorgo. Further on they saw the great River Ljunga flowing through a wide valley, the slopes clad in birches and aspen trees, a rich area with magnificent well-built farms.

"This is where the harvesters who mow the forest fields live," cried the eagle.

"It looks as if it pays to work in the forest," said Nils. "They're proper manor houses down there."

Gorgo swung east along the stately river. "That's the river which takes care of the crop and drives it to the mill."

Great masses of logs were floating down the river, but the boy could see no one taking care of it. Scarcely more than half the logs seemed to get where they were supposed to go. Perhaps the logs sailing along in the middle of the water did, but what happened to all the others that got caught up on the banks and were floating in the still waters of bays? Or the ones that got broken in the waterfalls or jammed against rocks and became great unsteady heaps?

"I wonder how long it takes for this crop to get to the mill," he said. Then he saw the loggers working with their boat-hooks, bold resolute men leaping from stone to stone in the rapids and running along the swaying heaps of logs as if walking on smooth ground. It was so exciting, Nils turned round backwards and watched them for a long time.

Gradually they came to the mouth of the river, where they saw a sawmill as large as a small town.

"That's the big timber mill called Svartvik," cried the eagle. "And over there is Sundsvall, the centre of the logging area."

They were very different from the towns in Skåne, which looked so grey and old and serious. Sundsvall was new and bright and radiant in a beautiful bay, a cluster of high stone buildings in the middle and in a curve round them wooden houses with little gardens.

"It's wonderful that it can look like this so far north," said the boy. "What an amazing country we have. Wherever I go, there's always something for people to live off."

The next day, they crossed the border into Ångermanland, and the boy could then see a river valley that surpassed every other one he had previously seen. It looked like three different worlds, Nils thought — furthest down in the valley timber-floating and salmon fishing, boats sailing and the sawmill clattering, then one storey higher up the valley farms and villages, the farmers sowing their patches, cattle grazing and the women weeding their kitchen gardens. And then highest up on the forested ridges, he saw the third world, where the capercaillie hen laid her eggs, the elk stood in the thick undergrowth, the lynx prowled round the squirrels raced about in the flowering bilberry scrub.

Suddenly the boy realized how hungry he was.

"I've had nothing to eat for two whole days," he complained. Gorgo had no wish for it to be said that things were worse for the boy with him than with the wild geese.

"You will have as much food as want. You don't have to starve with an eagle as your travelling companion." He spotted a farmer sowing his field, the seed in a sack on the edge of the field, so he headed for at that. But before he reached the ground, a tremendous uproar arose all round them. Crows and sparrows and swallows came in great numbers, screaming angrily at him because they thought the eagle was going to take a bird. Then when the farmer also came hurrying up, the eagle was forced to flee. The little birds mobbed him wherever he went and their cries made people come running out and chase him off. Nils felt quite sorry for Gorgo.

Then they came to a large farm where the mistress of the house had put a tray of freshly baked cinnamon buns out to cool. The eagle flew down but didn't dare approach right up to it. The farmer's wife saw him and laughed loudly.

"If you want a bun, come and take it!" she called, holding a bun up.

Nils sat in a pine top munching the delicious bun. If I become human again, he thought, I'll look up that nice woman by this great river and thank her properly.

Chapter 13

In the morning, the wind had been coming from the north, but now it had turned and was behind them. The journey was so calm it seemed as if they were quite still in the air. The coast of Västerbotten ran below them and the ground almost appeared to be moving beneath them. Had it perhaps got tired of standing still so far up north? Nils imagined the whole of Västerbotten marching south — a visit of that kind would certainly cause some raised eyebrows!

The eagle gradually increased speed.

"We're heading into Lapland now," he said. But Nils was disappointed when he saw nothing but mosses and forests, forests and mosses, and he grew so sleepy he almost fell off. Gorgo at once grabbed him in his claws and called out: "Falling asleep, Tom Thumb? The sun keeps me awake, so I go on in the night." He swung up into space, an elk looking at them in surprise, and although the boy was so uncomfortable, he nevertheless dozed off and was soon sound asleep.

When he woke, he was alone down in a large mountain valley. He got up and looked around, then saw a peculiar construction of pine branches up on a cliff ledge. "That must be the kind of eyrie Gorgo ..."

Before he had time to think the thought out, he snatched his cap off his head, swung it round and shouted hurrah. Gorgo had put him down in the valley where the eagle lived on the ledge and the wild geese were down in the valley. He was there!

Slowly, he walked on, looking for his friends. The whole valley was quite quiet, the sun not yet up over the edge of the cliff, so Nils Holgersson realized it was so early in the morning, the wild geese had not yet woken up.

Nils searched in the undergrowth and in crevices and found stranger geese as well as the wild geese from his own flock, but he didn't wake them. He thought he saw something white glimmering in some bushes and his heart started thumping with joy. Yes, it was true, there was Dunfin sitting on her eggs, the white gander beside her. Although he was asleep, it was clear he was proud to be standing guard over his wife in the mountains of Lapland.

Without waking him, the boy went on. Over on a little hill, he saw something like a grey tussock, and when he got closer he saw it was Akka from Kebnekajse standing on guard over the valley.

"Goodday, Mother Akka," called the boy. "How good that you're awake. Don't wake the others, because I want to talk to you alone."

The old leader goose rushed down the slope to meet the boy, at first grabbing him and shaking him, then stroking his back with her beak, then shaking him again, but quietly so as not to wake any of the others.

Nils kissed Mother Akka on both cheeks and told her how he had been taken to Skansen and how he had found Gorgo, pitiful and miserable in the eagle cage.

"At first I thought I'd file through the wire and let him out. But then I thought what a dangerous robber and bird-eater he is, so I thought it best that he stayed inside. Was that right of me, Mother Akka?"

"No, Nils, the eagles are prouder and greater lovers of freedom than most other creatures, and you can't keep them shut up. When you have rested, you and I will make a journey down to the bird prison and let him out."

"That's what I expected you to say, Mother Akka," said Nils happily. "Now I know that despite everything, you are fond of the one you brought up with so

70

much trouble. And if you want to thank whoever carried me here to you, then you'll find him up on the rocky ledge where you once found a helpless eaglet."

Nils Holgersson thought he had never been to such fair country and he had no worries except preventing the swarms of mosquitoes from eating him up. He saw little of Martin, as the great white gander's only thought was to stand guard over his Dunfin. But Nils stayed with Akka and Gorgo and they spent many happy hours with each other on long trips. Gorgo took him up to the peak of snow-capped Kebnekajse, where he could look down on the glaciers spreading out below the white cone, as well as the many other mountains seldom trodden by human feet. Akka showed him caves in the rock where the she-wolf brought up her cubs, and Torne Marsh where great herds of reindeer were grazing on the shores. He was also taken to meet the bears. And one day they flew to a small lake far away in the north. At the south end of the lake was a huge mountain massif called Krunavaara which appeared to consist entirely of iron ore, and on the other side a mountain equally rich in iron. They were building a railway up there, as well as a station and housing for all the workers and engineers who were to live there and extract the ore. Rock was being blasted, walls built, timber sawn, so a whole small town was beginning to emerge.

West of the lake the ground was open and free, and a Lapp family or two had struck camp there. All they had to do was to cut down a few osier bushes to make a clear space, and when they had fixed their tent poles into the ground and hung the tent on to them, their dwelling was ready. They had no more trouble over furnishing, a few spruce branches and reindeer skins on the floor and a chain fastened to the top of the tent poles for the iron pot to hang from when cooking their reindeer meat. The settlers in Kiruna had a great deal of work to do to get their houses ready before the hard winter came. They were surprised at the Lapps who had roamed around up there for centuries with no more protection against the cold and storms than thin tent walls. And the Lapps were surely equally surprised the settlers took so much trouble and worked so hard, when in order to exist no more was required than a few reindeer and a tent.

Yes, it was fine country. Nils was glad he had been allowed to see it, but he had no desire to live there for ever. No, he thought Akka was right when she said the settlers might just as well leave the countryside in peace to the bears, wolves and reindeer, and, of course, to the Lapps.

Chapter 14

Nils reckoned the time had come for the wild geese to go south, for the weather was beginning to break in the mountain valley. Rain, storms and thick mists alternated one after the other without ceasing and when it cleared, it was at once freezing cold. During the summer he had lived off berries and wild mushrooms, but now the berries had frozen and the mushrooms rotted, so he was finally forced to eat raw fish, which he did not like at all. The days grew much shorter, and it was rather boring with early evenings and late mornings for someone unable to sleep as long as the sun was out of the sky.

But it wasn't just because of the dark and cold and that food was short that he longed to get away from Lapland. He was longing to be back home with Martin the gander and to become human again.

One morning the ground was white as far away as he could see. The snow did melt later on in the day, and then Akka gave the signal for departure, for the wings of the young geese had grown out now and they could leave. Thirty-one geese flew south in an orderly skein, feathers fluttering and wings whipping the air with such a whistling you could hardly hear your own voice. Akka from Kebnekajse flew in the lead, followed by Yksi, Kaksi, Kolme and Neljä in one line, and Viisi, Kuusi, Dunfin and Martin with Nils on his back in the other, behind them the twenty-two young geese.

The poor young geese had never made a long trip before, so found it hard to keep up.

"Akka, Akka, Akka!" they lamented. "Our wings are tired out!"

"The longer you hold out the better it gets," said Akka, flying on as before. She must have been right, for after the young geese had flown for an hour or two, they no longer complained of tiredness. But they were used to eating all day and they started longing for some food. "Akka, we're so hungry!"

"Wild geese have to learn to eat air and drink wind," replied the leader goose, so they learnt to live off air, for after they had been flying for a while, they stopped complaining about being hungry. The old geese called out the names of all the mountain peaks so that the young ones would learn them.

"Porsotjollo! Sarjektjokko! Sulitelma!"

"Akka! Akka! We haven't room for all those names in our heads," the young geese complained.

"The more that gets into a head the more room there'll be in there," replied Akka, and she went on calling out those amazing names.

The boy was pleased when he saw the first pine forest, the first grey mountain farm, the first goat, the first cat, and he waved his cap and cheered.

The bears at Tännforsen growled to their cubs: "Look at that lot, so scared of a bit of cold, they daren't stay at home in the winter!" But the old wild geese had an answer for them: "Look at that lot, preferring to go to sleep for the whole winter rather than going to the trouble of going south!"

They kept meeting migrating birds flying in much larger flocks than in the spring.

"Where are you off to, wild geese?" they asked.

"Overseas, just like you, just like you," cried the geese.

Lapps and reindeer were also moving down from the mountains. Nils saw a herd trekking down with a Lapp in the lead, then the great bulls ahead of the others, after them the pack-reindeer with loads on their backs, and last of all ten or so Lapps behind. The wild geese cried out: "Thanks for this summer!"

And the reindeer replied: "Have a good journey and welcome back!"

Hardly had the wild geese called out that they were now flying into Jämtland when the mists came rolling in and hid their view, so the boy saw nothing of the journey, and in the evening the geese came down on a green hill where everything was soaking wet, drops hanging from every blade of grass, so as soon as Nils moved, he was given a shower.

He could just see a house so high it vanished into the mist and he realized it must be an outlook tower. No doubt he could lie in the dry up there, so he asked Martin to fly him up then fetch him again the next morning. But when he woke, the geese had gone and no one answered from the ground.

The boy was quite desperate. Once again he was separated from Martin and all kinds of things might happen to the gander on the journey.

Suddenly, Bataki was standing beside him. Nils never thought he would ever be so pleased to see the raven again.

"Akka sends her regards," said the raven. "She saw a hunter roaming about on the mountain and so didn't dare stay. But I will take you to your friends."

High above the mists, Bataki flew in brilliant sunlight, the wild geese nowhere to be seen, but that didn't worry the raven.

"I'll find them all right," he said. When the mists lifted, he came down on a stubble field by an old farm and the boy was able to search out a few grains for breakfast. After that they flew to a tree on the top of a ridge and sat on a branch each.

"I'm sure you don't know what kind of mound this is," said Bataki. "It's a burial mound and was made for the first man to settle in Härjedalen."

"Tell me about him, please," said Nils, munching on a grain of corn.

"I don't know much," said Bataki. "But he was a Norwegian called Härjulf. He quarrelled with the Norwegian king and so had to flee the country. He went to the Swedish king in Uppsala and was taken into his service. But then he wanted to marry the king's sister and when the king objected, Härjulf fled with her, which meant he was now in a position that he could live neither in Norway nor in Sweden, and he didn't want to go abroad. There must be another way out, he thought, so he took his wife and all his people into the great desolate forests north of Dalarna. There he cleared land and built a house, so became the first settler in this part of the country."

The raven fell silent and suddenly looked thoughtful. "As we are alone together …" he said in the end. "… I will ask you something. Do you really know what conditions the gnome made for you to become human again?

"I've heard nothing except I must bring the white gander back safe and sound again," replied the boy in surprise.

"I thought as much," said Bataki. "The last time we met, you spoke of how unpleasant it was to betray a friend, so you ought to know all of the conditions. Akka would perhaps prefer to help you rather than Martin the gander, but I think you will be grateful if you knew what the gnome said. Well, he said you will become human if you take the gander home so that your mother can slaughter him."

"The boy leapt up and almost fell to the ground. "You've just thought up that nasty idea!" he cried.

"Ask Akka," said the raven. "Look, there's the flock flying by. But don't forget there's always a way out of difficulties, as long as you can find it. It'll be fun to see whether you succeed."

The boy sat sullenly silent on the gander's back, his head hanging, not bothering to look around as they flew over Dalarna. I'll have to travel with the geese all my life, he thought, so I'll be seeing more than enough of this country. And he was no happier when the wild geese called out that they were now in Värmland and that the great river below was called the River Klar.

"I've already seen so many rivers and forests, that's enough," he muttered.

Before the wild geese had reached the long Lake Fryken, darkness had begun to fall. The moon came up, brilliant and round, and they flew down and settled on a wooded hill. The boy raced off to find something to eat and came to a road where a birch avenue opposite led up to a small manor farm. The house was surrounded by red rows of cottages and at the back was a leafy garden. Nils slipped inside and found so many delicious berries, he was quite dazed: red currants, gooseberries, raspberries and just imagine, a great big red apple lying there on the path!

He sat down beside it and cut off little slices with his knife. Being a gnome would be all right as long as there was always this kind of food to eat, he thought. Perhaps I should stay here? I don't know how to explain to Martin why I can't go home. Perhaps it'd be better if I kept away from him ...

At that moment, a horned owl flew down on to the path. "Nice to see a living creature," said the boy. "Can you tell me what this place is called, Mr Horned Owl?"

"The farm is called Mårbacka and you look like a nice tasty morsel," hissed the owl, fastening his claws into Nils' shoulder and pecking at his eyes. Nils realized his life was in danger and yelled for help as loudly as he could. Then he suddenly heard someone limping behind him and the owl let go and flew up into the nearest tree. An old lady was standing there shaking her stick at it.

"Thank you for your help," cried Nils. The lady looked rather surprised, so he went on: "I'm a human, just like you, but I've been turned into a gnome."

"That is the most amazing thing I've ever heard," said the lady. "How did you get into such a terrible mess?"

The boy told her everything that had happened and saw that she grew more and more astonished, amazed and pleased.

"What incredible good fortune I should come across you, who have ridden on the back of a goose all through the country. I was born here at Mårbacka and I like writing stories and sagas most of all. Then I thought it would be fun to tell a story about Sweden for all the school children, and a book suitable for schools has to be instructive and absolutely true. It turned out to be so difficult, I was just about to give up. But I can write just what you have told me into the book. You really have been a help!"

Chapter 15

After Fryksdalen, the wild geese flew straight over the wonderful woodlands of
Värmland, now brilliant in all their autumn colours, then across the long clear
blue lakes and their yellow shores. The boy was pleased to have been able to talk
to a human and the old lady had given him slight hope and confidence, which
must have been why he was able to think of a way to prevent the great white
gander from going home.

"Look, Martin, isn't it lovely?" he said. "I was just wondering whether we
oughtn't to go overseas together with the wild geese. It'd be a pity not to see
more of the world."

"You can't mean that seriously," said the horrified gander. He had just shown
that he was able to make a journey to Lapland and was now quite content to go
back to the goose-pen in Holger Nilsson's cowshed.

"I thought you wanted to show your mother and father what a clever boy
you've become, Tom Thumb," he went on. All summer Martin had been
dreaming of showing Dunfin and the goslings to all the other animals and to the
farmer's wife, so he was not particularly pleased with the boy's suggestion.

The wild geese then flew over the western part of Dalsland, where it was even
more magnificent than in Värmland, so many lakes, the land seemed to be high
banks between them and the steep shores like lovely parks with their bright red
aspen trees, creamy birches and reddish yellow rowans, the evening sun casting
streaks of gold across the dark waters.

"Don't you think it'd be a pity not to see more of all this glory?" said the boy.

"I'd rather have the rich fields at home in Söderslät," said the gander.

"Look, look Martin!" cried Nils again. "Have you ever seen anything like it!"
High up above the road, a large boat was gliding along a channel, and above
that ran a railway line, a train rushing along it, and just imagine, above that a
bridge with people looking down on it all.

"The Haverud aqueduct," called the older geese. "That's the Dalsland canal
running below us."

"You don't see things like that in Skåne," said Nils.

"Oh, well," said Martin. "If you simply must go on to see more peculiar things, then I suppose I'll have to go with you."

"I thought that'd be your answer," said the boy, and you could hear he considered his troubles now over.

As the geese flew over Bohuslän, he saw that the mountain ranges were now more coherent and the valleys like small crevices with gleaming black lakes at the bottom. The boy stared over at the bright streak that was the sea as it grew broader and broader until it was there, milky white and shifting in rose-red and sky-blue ahead of them, the great red sun just about to dive below the waves.

The boy had a great sense of peace and safety as he looked at the infinite open sea and the mild evening sun.

"Not worth getting upset," the sun was saying. "The world is a wonderful place to live in for both large and small. And it's good to be free and happy-go-lucky with the whole universe ahead of you."

Bohuslän resembled one long stone wall with some lush grass in the cracks, Nils thought. Here and there, the wall had collapsed and the sea was able to creep in into miles-long fjords, though it was just as well the magnificent archipelago lay beyond to take on the worst assaults from the sea and storms.

It must be different to live in Bohuslän, thought Nils.

The people of Bohuslän travel on roads they don't have to build or repair, can catch creatures no one has to herd or look after, and their boats are drawn by hauliers needing neither food nor stables. They have no fear of settling where there's hardly room for a potato patch, for they know the great wealth of the sea can provide them with all they need.

But the sea was also difficult to handle. Any man wishing to wrest something from it had to be knowledgeable in a great many ways and first and foremost be courageous and not be afraid of risking his life in the struggle against the waves.

As the wild geese flew down the coast the next morning, the small fishing villages and their brightly painted cottages were quiet and still, the brown nets hanging on the drying racks and blue and green boats, their sails furled, lay bobbing up and down in the harbours. The gutting benches were empty, and the pilot house closed. But suddenly a swarm of gulls set off at speed to the south, the cormorants following them in their plodding flight. The boy saw dolphins gliding through the sea like long black spools and a clump of seals humping their way down from a skerry. Then suddenly people were running around on the slippery flat stones in the fishing villages, the boats made ready and the dry seines carefully taken on board. Soon the water was full of brown and green sails.

"What's going on? What's going on?" asked the young geese, and a passing long-tailed duck replied: "The herring have come to Marstrand! The herring have come to Marstrand!"

The wild geese arrived at the wide fjord just as the shoal of herring poured in from the west. The men in the boats knew from the rippling and darkening of the water that the herring had stopped, so they put out their long seines in a circle, then tied them up at the bottom so the herring found themselves in an enormous sack. This was then drawn to and tightened until the glittering catch could be hauled out of the depths.

The men were standing knee-deep in herrings, fish-scales winking from sou'wester to the edge of their yellow oilskins. The people on land seemed delirious at the sight of all this silver hauled up out of the waves. The wild geese flew round several times so that Nils could see it all.

He also noticed more and more ships at sea, all apparently coming from or sailing towards a definite place.

"That's Gothenburg over there," cried Akka. And although the geese were flying high, Nils could see that it was a truly rich merchant city. He had never seen so many bright red-tiled and vivid green copper roofs before. Blue canals criss-crossed through the parks, leading out to the wide harbour that was the mouth of the River Göta and hundreds of ships were lying there along the kilometre-long quays. They would soon be out on all the seas of the world, overseas, just like Nils Holgersson.

Chapter 16

The wild geese took the route into Västergötland and came down on a large field in the neighbourhood of Falköping. They stayed there and had a happy time with other flocks of geese, though Nils was not so happy.

"If only I'd left Skåne behind me and was already in foreign parts, then I would know there was no longer anything to hope for ..." he said to himself.

A week or two later, they at last departed and headed over the Halland hills into Skåne. The boy hung over the gander's neck and raised his eyes. As he saw the plain spreading right over to the horizon, he was both pleased and anxious.

"I can't be far away from home now!" When he saw the first clump of willows and the first timber-framed house, his heart ached with homesickness.

During their midday rest, Akka came over to Nils.

"The weather's calm now, so I thought we'd cross the Baltic tomorrow," she said.

"Oh, mm," he said rather briefly, for his throat was so tight he was unable to speak, probably thinking the spell would be lifted from him after all.

"We're quite near Västra Vemmenhög," said Akka. "Perhaps you'd like to go home for a while to see them?"

"Better not," said Nils, but you could hear from his voice he was pleased with the suggestion.

"If the gander stays here with us, nothing can go wrong," said Akka. "You ought to find out how things are with them at home. Perhaps you can help them in some way, although you're small."

"Yes, you're right, Mother Akka, I ought to have thought of that before," he replied eagerly, and the next moment they were off. It wasn't long before Akka flew down behind the stone wall round Holger Nilsson's farm. Nils Holgersson quickly climbed up on to it.

"Just think, it's just the same. It seems like yesterday when I saw you flying in."

"Has your father a gun?" said Akka uneasily.

"Yes, of course, it was because of the gun I stayed away from church that Sunday," said Nils.

"Then I daren't wait for you. You'll have to come and meet me at Smygehuk early tomorrow morning."

"Oh no, don't go, Mother Akka." The boy sensed something was going to happen and they would never meet again.

"You've probably noticed I've been miserable because I can never be big again," he said. "But don't think I regret going with you. I'd rather remain a gnome than not have made this journey."

Akka drew several deep breaths before she answered: "You talk as if we were never to meet again, but we'll see each other tomorrow morning, won't we?" She stroked the top of Tom Thumb's head with her beak, then flew away.

The farm was quiet and there was no one in sight. Nils hurried to the cowshed, for he knew they would tell him what was going on.

Mayrose was alone inside, her head hanging. The boy ran fearlessly into her stall.

"Good-day, Mayrose! How are Mother and Father and all the rest of you on the farm?"

Mayrose started back and lowered her horns. Yes, he was just as small and wearing the same clothes as when he had left. But all the same, he was different, lively and agile, no longer a lazy dullard, his eyes bright and his stance jaunty. Mayrose was pleased to see him.

"Mooo!" she lowed. "Welcome home. They said you'd changed, but I didn't really believe it. Your parents have had nothing but sorrows since you went away, worst of all with the new horse. There's something wrong with him and no one can find out what. He can't work and they can't sell him. They had get rid of Star and Lily instead."

"I suppose Mother was sad when Martin flew away?" said the boy.

"Yes," said Mayrose, "but mostly because she thought you had stolen the gander and slipped away with him. Though I'll have you know, she grieves for you in the way you grieve for the loss of what is dearest to you."

The horse in the stable was so fine and handsome, Nils could hardly believe there was anything wrong with him.

"I've got a nail in my foot and it hurts so that I can't walk," the horse told him. "The doctor hasn't been able to find it, but if you could help me, I'd be very pleased. I'm really ashamed of standing here eating without doing any work."

"Thank goodness you're not really ill," said Nils. "I'll try to arrange for you to be cured. May I draw a little on your hoof?"

He had hardly finished when he heard his parents' voices out in the yard. Oh, how troubled they sounded!

"If that horse doesn't get better soon, I'll have to sell the farm," his father was saying.

"I wouldn't say anything if it weren't for the boy," sighed his mother. "But where will he go if he comes back poor and miserable, and we're not here? If only I had him back, I would ask for nothing else."

And Father agreed with her entirely.

The he went into the stable and Nils had to creep away and hide in a corner. As usual, Holger Nilsson picked up the horse's foot to try to find what was wrong.

"But what's this?" he said. "There's something scratched on the hoof. 'Take the nail out of his foot.' Yes, I do believe there's something sharp inside there."

As Father was busy with the horse and the boy was still hidden in the corner of the stable, another stranger came to the farm. It was Martin, who had been unable to resist the temptation to show his family what a good life time he had as

a tame goose, and was now walking proudly round the yard with them. As the door to the cowshed was open, he went inside with Dunfin and all six young geese in a long line behind him.

"Come and look at the goose pen! It's all right, not dangerous," he said. "Look, oats in the feeding trough."

But the geese had hardly reached the trough when the door of the goose pen slammed shut and the mistress of the house was standing outside putting the hook back on the hasp.

"Father! Come and look!" she called. "The gander's in the goose pen with seven wild geese!"

And I've found out what's wrong with the horse," said Father. "I think our luck has turned. But best of all is that we don't have to think Nils stole the gander."

"It's a pity, but we'll have to slaughter them this evening if we're to get them to town in time. It's Martinmas in a few days' time. Come and help me take them into the house."

A moment or so later, the boy saw Father carrying Dunfin and Martin under his arms and going into the house. The gander was screaming: "Tom Thumb! Come and help me!" just as he usually did when he was in danger, although he didn't know the boy was nearby.

Nils Holgersson heard him all right, but stayed where he was behind the stable door. He was hesitating because if Martin were killed, that would be an advantage to him — he hadn't given a thought to the gnome's conditions at that moment — but was thinking that he would have to show himself to Mother and Father if he were to save the gander. And he didn't want to do that. Things were hard enough for them anyhow, he thought. Do I have add to their sorrows?

But when the door of the cottage closed, Nils sprang to life, rushed across the yard, leapt up on the oak board at the foot of the doorway and into the porch. Out of habit, he kicked off his clogs and went over to the door. But then, as he was so reluctant to show himself to his parents as a little creature, he simply couldn't lift his hand to knock.

"Don't forget this is about Martin, your best friend *ever* since you were last here," he said to himself. He thought about everything he and the gander had gone through on frozen lakes and stormy seas and among dangerous predators. Then he felt gratitude and love in his heart and overcame his doubts and banged on the door so that it swung open.

When he saw the gander on the slaughtering bench, he cried out: "Mother, you mustn't touch the gander!" and at once Martin and Dunfin let out cries of delight, so he knew they were still alive.

And Mother also let out a cry of delight! "Oh, how big and handsome you've become!" she cried, letting go the gander.

The boy had not gone inside, but was still standing in the doorway, as if uncertain of his reception.

"Oh, thank heavens I have you back again," said Mother. "Come in! Come inside!"

"Oh, how welcome you are," said Father, incapable of uttering another word.

But Nils was still hesitating in the doorway, unable to understand why they were so pleased to see him, the way he was. But when Mother came and flung her arms round him and pulled him into the room, he realized what had happened.

"Mother! Father! I'm human again!" he cried.

Chapter 17

Early next morning, Nils
Holgersson was walking alone
along the shore east of Smygehuk
fishing village. He had tried to wake Martin,
but the great white gander had said not a word,
only thrust his head under his wing and fallen
asleep again.

Nils himself was still in a kind of delirium,
sometimes feeling like a gnome and sometimes
human.

It looked like it was going to be a lovely day and he
was pleased the geese would have such fine weather
for their crossing. The air was full of continuous lure
calls as one great flock followed another and Nils
smiled at the thought that no one knew what the
birds were calling to each other in the way that
he did. As long as they're not my geese leaving
without saying goodbye, he thought, placing
himself on the very edge of the shore so that they
would see him.

One flock was calling louder and flying faster
than all the others, then they slowed down and kept
flying back and forth, searching. The boy saw that it
was his, but why didn't they land beside him? He
heard Akka calling, but couldn't make out what she
was saying. What was going on? Had the geese
changed languages?

He tried out the call that would bring them to him,
but, just imagine, his tongue wouldn't work!
He couldn't get out the right sound.

He waved his cap, shouted and ran, but that simply frightened them, so they flew out to sea. Then at last he understood. They hadn't recognized him. They didn't know he was human and unable to call them to him, because a human cannot speak the language of the birds.

But then he heard a great rush of wings. Akka had felt badly about leaving Tom Thumb, and had returned just once more. As the boy was sitting quite still, she dared to come closer, for someone had presumably opened her eyes to who he was. She settled down in the sand beside him.

The boy was radiantly happy and took old Akka in his arms. The other wild geese also came and rubbed their beaks against him and crowded round him. They cackled and chattered and wished him all the best and he thanked them for the wonderful journey he had been allowed to make in their company.

But when he spoke to them, the geese became strangely quiet and retreated from him, as if to say: "Ah, here is a human being! He doesn't understand us, and we don't understand him ..."

Then the boy rose to his feet and went over to Akka. He patted her and stroked her neck. Then he walked across the shore towards the land because he knew that the sorrow of birds does not last long and he wanted to part from them while they were still sad because they had lost him.

On the bank of the shore, he turned round and watched the flocks of birds flying over the sea, calling out their lure calls. Only one flock was flying in silence as far as he could follow them with his gaze.

The skein was even and orderly, their speed good, their wingbeats strong and powerful. The boy felt such a longing for the departing birds that he almost wished he were again Tom Thumb, who could ride over land and sea with his flock of wild geese.

så tragisk

der kan väl förklaras för den. Jag sänder afskrifter, som äro myckafvade.

Jag har skickat Dalin några nya förslag till tit-
lar. Vi vill inte ha mitt
"En resa öfver Sverige eller
En färd öfver Sverige. Jag vill
inte ha Boken om Sverige.
Vi ska väl till sist finna
något som är så slående
bra, att vi alla bli nöjda.
I Tyskland kalla de boken
"Nils Holgersons underbara
resa".

och jag tycker att detta
låter mycket tilltalande men
jag har också andra förslag.
med hjärtlig helsning
Er tillgifna
Selma Lagerlöf

Selma Lagerlöf

When Selma Lagerlöf was asked in 1901 whether she would participate in a new reader for elementary schools, she was forty-three years old and a renowned and much liked author. In her first novel, *The Saga of Gösta Berling*, she had already demonstrated her narrative talent. She had grown up with the sagas and legends of her childhood Värmland and she incorporated that lively colourful language into her own writing. She was also a trained teacher and had worked in schools for ten years before deciding to devote herself to writing. So it was natural for teachers to turn to her for contributions to the new reader. A committee had been appointed, and a plan of what the reader should contain had been thoroughly worked out. But when, after some hesitation, Selma Lagerlöf accepted, she took the matter into her own hands. She wanted to abandon disconnected little stories and verses. She wanted to write the whole book herself as a coherent story, a truly exciting saga that would also contain the geography of Sweden and make children aware of their country and people.

Selma Lagerlöf did a great deal of preparatory work. She made several journeys, read many books, including some on geography and zoology, and she also received suggestions and opinions from various quarters. As a child, she had already been an voracious reader and for her world literature was a treasure to be plundered, which also left traces in her story. But despite her wealth of material, she found it hard to find the right form for her book, and the work was delayed. When she finally found the right solution, the writing of it went amazingly quickly. Rudyard Kipling's *Just So Stories* gave her the idea, the animals humanized in speech and thought, but nevertheless following their own natural behaviour. In the same way, Selma Lagerlöf wished to give character to her creatures, and through them describe various events and places. The best overall picture one could have, of course, was a bird's eye view over Sweden, and that required a little fellow to make the journey: Nils Holgersson.

The manuscript was read by a number of teachers and other experts, who all made comments in the margins, and now and again Selma was extremely annoyed. But she nonetheless made some alterations, and she was extremely thorough in making sure all the factual information was correct. The revision was a laborious task, not least because so many people wanted a finger in the pie.

The first part about Nils Holgersson's journey in the five southernmost regions came out in 1906, and the second part the following year. They were received with acclaim and shortly afterwards a slightly amended version of the story was brought out in one volume. New editions are still being printed today. The book is translated into over thirty languages and is read all over the world.

The saga of Nils Holgersson is no longer used as a school reader, but it has become no less readable for that. Selma Lagerlöf's strong sense of the richness of nature and her involvement in it are a source of inspiration at a time when it is a matter of urgency to care for the environment and value what nature provides. She describes a countryside which today belongs in the past but just because of that is important to preserve in the memory. Through Lars Klinting's illustrations, as full of light, air and movement as the story itself, new generations of children can happily follow Nils Holgersson on his wonderful journey.

Rebecca Alsberg

Norway

Härjedalen

Dalarna

Hälsingl

Bohuslän

Värmland

Dalsland

Denmark

Västermanland

Gästrikland

Västergötland

Närke

Uppland

Halland

Östergötland

Södermanland

Småland

Skåne

Blekinge

Öland

Gotland